Ωmega Rising

Joshua Dalzelle

© 2013

Paperback Edition

*****

Edited by Monique Happy Editorial Services
www.indiebookauthors.com

Chapter 1

Jason Burke bolted upright in his bed and scanned the room. All was as he had left it and everything appeared as it should: dark and quiet. He was sweating profusely and his hands were clenched into fists. As he forced himself to breathe slow, regular breaths, his heart rate began to drop and he slowly calmed himself. Another nightmare. That was the only explanation as to why he was in such a state. They were becoming less and less frequent as time passed, but every once in a while he would still be violently awakened by ghosts from his past.

He knew it was of no use trying to get back to sleep so he swung his legs over the edge of the bed, groaning softly as he stood up. He padded across the bedroom and into the bathroom, his feet making no noise on the rough-hewn wood floor. He flipped on the light and splashed some water onto his face to clear his head. He gasped slightly as the icy water hit his skin; this far up in the mountains the well water was still very cold in early May. He looked up and stared at the man looking back at him in the mirror. That man had a fairly plain face, not overly handsome, but certainly not unattractive. An unruly crop of coarse, dark hair stuck out in places and looked like it hadn't been cut in months. There was three days' worth of beard growth that covered mildly weathered skin which bespoke of long durations in harsh environments and gave the twenty-six-year-old the appearance of someone a bit older. The light blue-almost grey-eyes stared back with an intensity that made him seem standoffish to strangers, yet there was a vulnerability there that few saw, and a sadness as well.

Jason shook his head in disgust. Too much introspection was never healthy. He turned the light off and walked back across his bedroom to the window and looked out over the moonlight-drenched mountains. The view was breathtaking but he hardly noticed it. Convinced that a recurring nightmare had been what woke him, he decided to try and sleep at least a few more hours. He fervently hoped the sheets weren't too sweaty.

He then became aware of a low, sub-sonic thrum as he sat back on the bed. He stuck his finger in his ear and wiggled it furiously, not actually expecting the act to stop the noise but figuring it was worth a try. The sound was more a feeling but it was growing in intensity. Within the next few minutes he confirmed that the noise was indeed real, and not in his head, as the panes of glass in his bedroom window started to vibrate. Jason stood back up and approached the window as the sensation continued to climb in pitch and volume until it broke into the audible range. Whatever it was, it was getting closer. He dashed out of his bedroom, ran down the stairs, and went to the back door that led out onto the rear deck of the cabin. He paused long enough to slip on a leather coat and put on a pair of leather-soled moccasins before opening the door and stepping out into the cold night air.

He stepped to the far rail and craned his head towards where the sound was coming from, listening as the low rumble became accompanied by a high-pitched whine. Just when he thought whatever was making the cabin shake would pass out of his line of sight, a roaring sound made him jump as what looked like a low-flying comet streaked across the night sky and disappeared over the next ridge. He jumped again as the sound of an explosion reached him and the horizon lit up where the object had passed. But unlike an explosion, the sound and light did not dissipate. The incredible roar actually increased and shook the mountain as Jason gripped the deck railing so hard his knuckles turned white.

Then it was over. The silence was deafening and only the moon lit up the night. Jason stood stock still, staring at the spot where the object had disappeared. His breathing was quick and shallow and his eyes scanned the ridgeline for any sign of movement. Something was very wrong. He had caught a glimpse of the object as it crossed the sky; it was definitely some sort of aircraft and it had been trailing fire and billowing smoke as it screamed over his cabin. But it had been unlike any aircraft he had ever seen or heard of, even from his time in the military. His instincts told him that this was no ordinary aviation mishap. The long duration of the explosive roar after the craft had flown over was simply not consistent with an aircraft impacting the ground and exploding.

Jason ran back into his cabin and picked up the land line—his cell phone was useless this far up in the mountains—and was greeted by more silence. The line was dead. With only a moment's hesitation he went upstairs and quickly dressed in old fatigue pants, boots, and pulled a hoodie sweatshirt over his t-shirt. The night was cold, but he knew he'd be moving fast enough to stay warm without a coat. He hesitated momentarily, then the last thing he grabbed from his bedroom was an AR-15 carbine from the corner of the closet and a loaded 30-round magazine from the top shelf. He knew he may very well be a paranoid fool, but something about this didn't sit well with him and the weapon gave him a sense of security.

He paused again at the back door and grabbed a small, high-intensity flashlight and stuffed it in his front pocket and slipped his wallet into his back pocket. He slapped the magazine into the rifle's lower receiver, grabbed the charging handle and cycled the weapon's action, loading a live round into the chamber. He verified it was on "safe" and slipped outside. Jason closed the door without a thought of locking it; there was nobody within miles of the small cabin, one of the main reasons he was hiding out in it.

He hopped off the porch and headed down a well-worn trail that led into the woods. His familiarity with the land allowed him to move quickly through the pine trees with only the light of the moon to illuminate his path. He judged that the aircraft (or, most likely, the crash site) was no more than two or three klicks away given the speed it was traveling and the time from when he lost sight to when the sound had stopped.

He had no idea what he expected to see when he got there, so he mentally prepared himself for anything and everything.

The easy, loping gait Jason assumed was good for covering distances relatively quickly without leaving him worn out when he arrived. The few kilometer run, even through the rugged mountain terrain, wasn't much of a challenge to him. The AR-15, a civilian version of the military M4 rifle he had trusted his life to many times, was a comforting weight in his hands as he jogged, holding it across his chest. As he ran he could feel the subtle change from the drowsy, relaxed demeanor he had adopted in the small mountain town he lived in to a brittle alertness that had been finely honed by multiple combat tours in Iraq and Afghanistan. Nothing escaped his attention; every sound and shadow was scrutinized and catalogued as he ghosted through the wilderness towards his destination.

Soon there was a discernable brightness along the ridgeline up ahead so Jason slowed to a walk and then eventually stopped. He crouched down on the soft earth and strained his ears for any sound that wasn't natural. The light was definitely artificial, however faint it was. The hue and brightness told him the light was not coming from a natural source, and the steady, constant glow was also inconsistent with flaming wreckage, the thing he most expected to find. He began a silent stalk the remaining distance up to the ridge and paused right below the crest of the hill. He could now hear and feel a dull thrum coming from the area as well as the occasional sound that he could only describe as mechanical. Why was he so wired and apprehensive over what was most likely an aviation mishap? Whatever the reason, he had learned long ago not to shrug off the feeling; it was a lesson that had nearly cost him his life.

The last five meters to the top of the ridge were made at a snail's pace as Jason crawled on his elbows and the toes of his boots, the AR-15 cradled protectively in his arms. He knew this area well from months of scouting out from his cabin and knew there was a large clearing up ahead, the soil being too rocky for the trees to take hold. The clearing sloped gradually west from his current position and ended in another tree line before butting up against the next rise. His crawl ended right before his line of sight would clear the ridgeline and he'd be able to see down into the clearing. At this point, the light was quite bright and the sounds of metal scraping on metal and the occasional clanking were clear as a bell. Jason hunched his shoulders forward and dug his elbows into the soil, then slowly used his shoulders and back to drag himself up the last little bit so he could get a clear view of his objective.

Although he wasn't sure what he had expected to see, the view stunned him nonetheless. The clearing was dominated by what was clearly an aircraft of some type, but it was unlike any he had ever seen or even heard of. For starters, it was simply huge. Jason had seen C-5 Galaxy cargo aircraft during his time in the service, but the craft currently sitting in front of him would easily dwarf the Air Force's largest plane. Despite its size, Jason was also certain he was looking at a tactical vehicle and not some slow, ungainly cargo hauler. The craft appeared to be an elongated delta shape from his vantage point above and behind it. There were discernable wings that extended out from the main fuselage, but the sweep maintained the same angle that started at the nose, far too steep a rake for normal flight. There were also what appeared to be two stabilizers extending out from the tail section at forty-five degrees, but even with his rudimentary knowledge of aerodynamics Jason could see that their orientation in relation to the wing would make them nearly useless at controlling the pitch of the craft, as well as probably adversely affecting the wing's performance. There were four engine nozzles that were arranged in pairs in two nacelles tucked up under the wing roots at the tail of the aircraft, but instead of the expected stream of hot gas Jason would normally expect from a gas turbine, a passive, wavering blue glow was pulsating down the visible length of the interior of the engines.

There were some other details that also stayed Jason's first instinct to race down the hill and render aid to any possible survivors, reasons in addition to the size and configuration of it. The aircraft (a word Jason insisted on still using to describe the behemoth in the clearing) was obviously damaged—badly—and it also had obviously landed, not crashed. Even from his position, he could tell the thing was sitting on its landing gear, but what threw him was *how*. A vehicle this large with such a swoopy, fast design should not be able to land vertically in an uneven, rough mountain clearing that could barely contain it. Or land vertically at all, for that matter. There was also the speed at which the craft had buzzed his cabin; it had been subsonic, but just barely, and it was streaming flames and smoke at the time, apparently a result of the damage he was looking at. This meant that even with that damage, the craft had managed to stop its considerable forward velocity and descend safely in a controlled landing. He realized that this must have been the sustained, explosive roar he had heard on his back porch: it had to have some type of incredibly powerful retro-thrust system. Jason's mind boggled at the amount of thrust it would take for the giant craft to hover and control its vertical decent, let alone stop it in midair. He moved his AR-15 into position and peered through the scope to get a better view. Even with the relative low magnification of the small tactical scope, he could clearly see much of the damage. Scorch marks were visible on the left side of the upper fuselage and there appeared to be impact damage in that area as well as a possible breach in the skin. While large aircraft looked tough and rugged, Jason knew they were relatively fragile objects and it occurred to him that there could still be injured crew on board this one.

He was the type of person who didn't waste time on indecision, so once he determined his course of action, he set about aggressively executing it and didn't expend any energy on regrets or contemplation about things he couldn't go back and change. He slowly slid himself out from his hiding spot and began a methodical descent down the steep hill towards the mysterious craft that was smoking and hissing before him. He knew it was probably smarter to haul ass back to his home and try to find some way to alert the authorities, but he couldn't resist the excitement of it. He was sure this was no experimental aircraft for the U.S. military. Well, mostly sure. But beyond that, he was unsure as to what this was that had blown away his peace and quiet. It couldn't really be an airplane, could it?

He descended the slope rapidly, using the trees for both cover and support to keep his speed in check. While he was still concerned about stealth, he knew the still-running engines from the craft should mask the sound of the loose dirt and scrub he was kicking up as he slid/hopped down the hill. He paused at the edge of the clearing and dropped to a knee. Holding perfectly still, he strained his ears and eyes to detect any trace of movement that indicated he had been detected. He was still obeying that extra sense that told him the utmost caution was required. He took off towards the craft at a crouched, loping gait that covered the gap quickly but didn't leave him breathless when he reached it. *What in the hell am I doing here?* The first twinges of real fear entered his mind as he approached to within twenty meters of the thing and realized just how large and *alien* it really was.

He stood under the left engine nacelle and looked around at the underbelly of the huge aircraft. The landing gear was the traditional tricycle type he was accustomed to: each strut ending in a dual-axle beam that was supported by a total of four wheels per assembly. Or at least they looked like wheels of a sort. They were spherical and obviously attached to the landing gear assemblies, but there were no visible fasteners or hubs that he could see. He peered around, unsure what his next course of action should be. He had rushed under the craft mostly on impulse. Now he wasn't sure what, exactly, he had hoped to accomplish. Just then, the aft section of the underbelly dropped a foot or so and rapidly lowered to the ground accompanied by the unmistakable whine of a hydraulic pump. After Jason had recovered from the sudden shock, he saw that the section of the skin between the engine nacelles had actually pivoted downward rather than lowered. It was a ramp.

Without thinking, Jason rushed towards the lowered end and came around the edge, raising his rifle halfway up as he did so without even realizing it. Nobody was there. The ramp led up into a well-lit bay that he couldn't see into from his position at the bottom of the ramp. Shrugging slightly to himself, he walked up the ramp. Hell, he had committed this far to an idiotic course of action, he may as well see it through to the end. Once at the top of the ramp, he found himself standing in the mouth of a large cargo bay. It was both familiar and somehow not. On one hand, it looked very much like the interior of a C-17 cargo jet; even the spars lining the walls that curved upwards into an arch very much looked like countless other aircraft he had been in. But on the other hand, there were some unsettling differences. The spars and the floor, for example, looked to be far too heavily built to be for any conventional aircraft. That, and the area was too sterile; it was completely void of the wire harnesses and machinery that littered the interior of any cargo plane he had ever been on.

His inspection was cut short when two louvered vents on the forward bulkhead opened and the interior of the cargo bay was suddenly transformed into a wind tunnel. Jason dropped to one knee and grabbed a tie-down point with his left hand while his right maintained control of his weapon. He closed his eyes and grimaced in agony from the overpressure as the air velocity continued to increase and an acrid smell began to fill the area. He opened his eyes and saw the vents were now belching out a thick, noxious smoke. His throat and eyes were on fire as he turned and tried to safely exit the cargo bay. Mercifully, the violent rush of air and smoke died down as suddenly as it had started. Coughing and streaming mucus, he only wanted to get down the ramp and into the fresh air he knew was just outside.

He turned back around just in time to see the ramp raise and lock and a set of interior doors slide around into place. He felt his ears pop from the pressure change and knew he was sealed in. Unfortunately, so were a good amount of the fumes from the vents. He was quickly losing consciousness so he couldn't tell if the floor was actually moving or not. *Climbing into this thing may have been a tad impulsive.* Even through his tunneled vision and detached perception, he was still surprised when the floor heaved and threw him into the rear doors.

Chapter 2

The blackness started to become gray.

Jason swam towards the light as his concussed brain struggled to restart all his cognitive functions. The gray tunnel he was looking though wavered and then coalesced into the deck plates of a C-17's cargo bay. But something was wrong about the metal surface his face was planted into. He lifted his head as his brain began to get feedback from the rest of his body: it hurt. Everywhere. His training overrode his panic and he lay still and began to systematically flex muscle groups to find out if, and where, he was injured. To his relief, the only true injury was his little finger on the left hand; it was severely dislocated. It hurt like hell, but he was still mobile.

He smoothly rolled to his side and got to his knees. Every part of his body screamed in pain, but he ignored it. He blinked his eyes and shook his head side to side to chase away the grogginess. *Ah, yes ... the "aircraft."* Other than his finger, which was sticking out at an unnatural angle, he appeared to be only slightly bruised and battered from his impact with the rear doors of the cargo bay. The lights in the hold were now dimmed considerably from when he'd first made entry, but he could still see well enough to move about. The next thing he noticed after his injuries was a conspicuous lack of weight in his hands. While he would normally be humiliated for losing control of his weapon, right then he was so confused as to what he had gotten himself into that he was not especially concerned with the normal operator bravado, doubly so since there was nobody there to see him anyway.

Climbing to his feet, he saw the AR-15, sans magazine, against the starboard wall of the cargo hold. Even as he was moving to retrieve the rifle, he was scanning the room for the magazine that must have ejected on impact. It took him a few more minutes to find the black polymer magazine, and when he saw it he feared the worst. If it had broken, he would be down to a single round in the chamber and he was now half convinced he had gotten himself into a situation that he may have to shoot his way out of. Happily, the magazine appeared to have suffered no ill effects from the abuse save for some superficial scratches. He slapped the mag back into the rifle and again felt ready to make some moves, even though his finger really, *really* hurt.

Jason's only priority at that point was to get out of the craft and make it back out of the area unseen. He has already gotten more than he'd bargained for during his ill-planned rescue attempt; he would clear the area and try again to alert the authorities. As he approached the rear doors, he could tell something was different. When he had first entered, there were the normal noises one would associate with that environment: air handlers, machinery humming, and the occasional high-pitched whine of a hydraulic accumulator charging. All these things were still present, but now there was a low-pitched rumble that drowned out all the other sounds, and it wasn't the noise Jason would typically associate with turbine engines. Although a part of his mind was cataloguing all of these anomalies, he didn't let anything distract him from his goal. In this case, his goal was the control panel mounted in a pedestal on the right side of the door that looked to be a likely location for the door/ramp controls.

When he reached the pedestal that he assumed controlled the rear doors, he was brought up short. If he still had any doubts that this was an American aircraft, they were confirmed by the panel's display. The symbols on the screen were definitely written words, but it was not in any language Jason recognized. That wasn't necessarily saying a lot; he only spoke English. He tentatively touched the display to see what would happen. He was rewarded with the display turning red and a short blast from a klaxon-style horn. Some more odd script scrolled across the screen and then it went dark. Subsequent touches on the panel elicited no reaction.

Fantastic. Now what? He turned back to look at the front bulkhead to see what other options he might have.

There were two doors in the forward bulkhead of the cargo bay. One was at deck level and was large and very heavily built. The second door looked like the typical interior hatch you would see on a naval surface vessel, ovoid in shape and slightly inset into the bulkhead. It was directly over the first, larger door and accessible by a walkway and a staircase that ran down the port side of the cargo bay. The lower door looked well-secured but the upper door looked like a standard crew access hatch. With the same lack of thinking that had gotten him into the situation in the first place, he moved decisively towards the staircase and the upper access hatch.

He stood before the hatch and couldn't find an obvious handle to open it. He did, however, see a large red, circular button. Doing what humans instinctually do when confronted with a large red button, Jason pressed it. Thankfully, the hatch simply slid aside into the wall recess giving Jason easy access to the interior of the craft. He peered into the doorway, rifle at the ready, but there was nothing to see except a dark passageway. *Of course it has to be dark.* He was beginning to be less and less comfortable about his situation, if that was even possible. Everything seemed ... off. Even the act of walking had an odd feel to it.

Remembering he had slipped his flashlight into his pocket, he grabbed it and lit up the area just beyond the hatch. It was rather anti-climactic; there was nothing but a short passage with a touchscreen control panel on the wall displaying that same indecipherable language as in the cargo bay, and another entry hatch at the far end. As he crossed the threshold of the hatchway, the flashlight slipped out of his hand and hit the deck. He froze instantly. That was *definitely* not right. There was a barely perceptible delay from when he expected the light to hit the floor and when it actually did.

Frowning, he grabbed the charging handle of his rifle and cycled the action with the ejection port facing up. The cartridge flipped up and out of the rifle as it should, but seemed to take too long to hit the deck, and it flew further than he would have expected as well. *What the hell is happening?* He hopped lightly on the balls of his feet and he felt different, lighter. He again looked at the bizarre, alien language scrolling on the display to his right. His mind shied away from an obvious, yet absurd conclusion.

He moved toward the second hatch, pausing to retrieve the ejected round and slip it into his pocket, and was relieved/horrified to find that the hatch automatically cycled to allow him further entry. *An airlock?* He gripped his rifle and moved forward with a determined scowl on his face. He desperately wanted off this ship (the word had automatically begun to replace "aircraft" in his mind) and get back to his cabin without being seen. He had the distinct feeling that no matter how noble his intentions were, his intrusion would likely be a punishable offense.

As he traversed further into the ship's interior, he noticed the unmistakable smell of burning avionics. He had been first on the scene at enough crashes to have the unique smell of burning wire, circuit boards, and composites permanently etched into his brain. The widening passageway he was in had a definite haze in the air that was visible in the low-level lighting that looked to be some type of emergency lighting rather than a primary light source. Jason pressed on, wondering when he would run into the first crew member of this ship. He was still clinging desperately to the belief that this was a heretofore unknown craft built in secret by a foreign nation that had happened to crash land in his backyard. But the evidence was mounting that this may not be the case; the technology evident here seemed far beyond anything he had ever heard of, and then there was the written language scattered throughout the interior. *Maybe all that Area 51 bullshit was no joke.*

As the corridor ended, Jason could see the interior was laid out around a large, open center area that looked to have some common spaces and what appeared to be computer terminals along the left side. The right side was dominated by what had to be the galley, judging by the high-top metal table and sterile looking counters. There were additional hatches interspersed along the bulkheads, and the center aisle he was standing in continued all the way forward to a wide staircase that led up into another darkened corridor from which emanated a dim, red glow. After affirming that the large main area he was standing in was empty, Jason strode quickly for the stairs ahead of him. He was operating under the assumption that *whoever* built this thing also put the flight deck at the front. As he passed a lounge area, he noted that the furniture looked like standard, Earthling furniture. That was somewhat comforting, but did little to stave off Jason's rising anxiety.

Jason walked up the stairs with purpose, actually shouldering his weapon and making sure he was ready for anything, safety off. While he had no hostile intentions, he also had no desire to walk flat-footed and helpless into a bad situation. The corridor at the top of the stairs wasn't especially long or wide, but at the end he could make out the telltale sign of indicator lights and heard a soft muttering that he couldn't make out, punctuated by what he assumed were beeps from the instruments. He stalked forward on silent feet, ready for anything. He noted three rooms off the corridor, two to the left and one to the right, but they were unoccupied. That was as far as his investigation went; his goal was just in sight and he wouldn't be deterred by poking around in empty rooms.

Flattening himself against the bulkhead at the threshold of the flight deck, Jason took a quick, cleansing breath and let it back out silently. In one fluid motion he rolled around the edge and brought his weapon to bear. The flight deck was enormous and was dominated by an incredible wrap-around canopy that blended with the contours of the ship. He noticed it was divided into four main sections. The view outside, however, riveted Jason where he stood and sent his panic reflex into overdrive. Right outside, in all her glory, was the unmistakable sight of Saturn, up close and personal.

"Oh shit!"

That was all he got out before he noticed movement to his right. He whipped his head around and was face to face with … *Is that a fucking robot!?* The … thing … looked at him with an equally surprised expression. Its face looked like some sort of dull, burnished metal that flexed like skin and the eyes were surprisingly organic-looking. That was as far as he got. The "robot" assumed an exasperated expression (*What the hell?!*) and spoke to the ceiling in an unknown language: the disdain in its voice was unmistakable. There was a bright flash and a burst of pain that felt like a taser strike all over his body. Darkness once again washed over him. He wondered what the incredibly loud *CRACK!* was just before his face impacted the deck.

Chapter 3

Ah damn, what the hell happened? I feel like a truck ran me over.

Jason pried one eye open against the pain he felt everywhere. More pain. A bright, intense white light pierced through the cracked eyelid and rode the optic nerve straight to the pain center in his brain. He quickly slammed the eye shut but now noticed the bright red glow as the overhead light shone through the skin of his lids. Still a trained warrior before anything else, he began to take stock of his injuries and situation before wasting time wondering where, exactly, he was. As best he could tell, the pain was generalized and intense, but not the result of a specific injury. He just hurt like hell everywhere. He could tell he was lying on his back on a fairly comfortable surface and that he was restrained. This last fact alarmed him greatly, although he did remember that he had stormed the flight deck, uninvited, brandishing a weapon. At this last thought his eyes popped open. Saturn. The robot. The written script throughout the ship.

"I'm on an alien spaceship," he said aloud to nobody, or so he thought.

"Actually, you're the alien in this case, and you're on my ship." Jason's heart nearly stopped at the voice. He craned his head to the left and down and saw the robot standing at the foot of the platform he was strapped to. He was able to take in more detail of the strange machine than he had been able to when first confronted by it. The face, made of that exotic, flexible metal, was oddly human-like, but without ears or a nose.

"What?!" It was the best he could do as his brain struggled to keep up. Of all the questions he could have asked a being from another world, there was only one thing that he could think of. "How are you speaking English?" The robot's face morphed into an expression of incredulity, complete with a cocked brow. He was once again stunned at how familiar the gestures and expressions were.

"You're strapped to an infirmary bed on a ship from another world while, presumably, being the first of your kind to lay eyes on the planet we're currently orbiting. That was the question that was most on your mind? Truly?" The sarcasm that laced the voice told Jason he was not dealing with a simple automaton. The pain in his head increased as he simply couldn't keep his panic reflex under control. His heart rate began to climb quickly. Being restrained and, apparently, abducted was simply too much for his brain to process, so it didn't bother trying and he promptly fainted. The robot walked over to peer down at Jason. Looking at one of the displays on the wall, it shrugged and walked back out of the infirmary.

The second time Jason awoke strapped to the same infirmary bed he felt much better, albeit still quite confused. He had no recollection of time, but it seemed like it must have been at least twelve hours since he had first boarded the ship. The sensation distressed him greatly. Years of military training and experience had honed his internal chronometer to such a degree of accuracy that he never needed an alarm clock anymore; he simply decided when he should wake up and he would. Well, give or take a quarter of an hour. He concentrated on the passage of time. It distracted his mind from the reality of the situation, something he really didn't want to deal with just yet. Instead, he once again began to take a mental inventory of his body by systematically flexing muscle groups. He frowned. Maybe he'd been out far longer than he thought. He couldn't detect so much as a strained muscle. In fact, he felt better than he had in years. When he finally moved it was to lift his head and look down at his body. As soon as he did he heard a *beep beep* and the restraints released and retracted into the base of the bed he was laying on. *Interesting.*

He sat up and swung his legs over the side of the bed. Sitting there, he took in the room he found himself in. While intellectually he knew he must be aboard an alien spacecraft after seeing Saturn right outside and talking to what he assumed to be a robot, part of him still refused to deal with the enormity of it all. His trained operator's mind still insisted on thinking tactically rather than existentially.

There!

On a counter to his right was the intimately familiar buttstock of his AR-15. *Maybe they don't know what it is?* They. Even though he hadn't seen another animated soul other than the tin man on the flight deck, he had to assume that there was something ... else ... on board this ship. He stood slowly, half expecting an alarm to sound or a restraint to latch onto him. As soon as he stood his heart dropped. The rifle had been field stripped and its guts lay neatly organized across the metallic surface. The AR's parts were not alone. The rest of his possessions were also laid out in a similar fashion; his wallet, for example, had its contents in rows beside it.

Displaying the same single-mindedness that had landed him in his current debacle, he strode over and began reassembling the weapon. Less than a minute later he was cycling the action to verify everything was back where it should be. When he grabbed the magazine he stopped; it weighed only a few ounces in his hand: empty. The aliens weren't as ignorant as he'd hoped. Remembering something, he thrust his hand into the front pocket of his pants. No luck. They'd grabbed the loose round he had stuck in there as well. Even though it was now little more than a fancy-looking club, he just couldn't leave the firearm behind. Sighing, he put the assembled weapon down and began collecting the rest of his stuff.

The flashlight had been left unmolested and after a quick check to ensure it was functional, he stuffed it into his pocket. He started putting everything back into his wallet when he paused at a worn photograph. Picking it up reverently, he gazed at the beautiful blond woman smiling back at him. She was wearing cutoff jean shorts and a black t-shirt, and was leaning over the open door of an older red Camaro, her eyes sparkling. He flipped it over and read the name written on the back, complete with a little heart drawn after it. He turned it over again and looked at the photo for a moment longer. Setting his jaw, he slipped the photo into the back of his wallet and ignored the hollow ache in his chest.

He walked towards the glass doors that looked much like the doors you would see leading into a supermarket on Earth. Like their Earthling counterpart, the doors slid apart with an electric whine and he stepped through to find himself in the large common area he had traversed earlier on his way to the flight deck. *Is it a flight deck, or a bridge? Eh, who gives a shit.* Looking left, he saw the stairs that led up to the flight deck and walked towards them without hesitation. He deduced that if whoever owned this ship wanted him dead, he'd have been dead well before now, so he strode up the stairs with no regard given to stealth and walked with what he hoped was a confident swagger onto the flight deck again.

"Oh excellent. You're up and about again. Any other brilliant questions you'd like to ask?" The robot's voice came from the front of flight deck near an access panel close to the enormous canopy.

"My name is Jason Burke. May I ask why I'm here?" Jason felt being polite yet direct was his best bet. The robot turned from the open panel and gave him an incredulous look.

"You're here because you took it upon yourself to board this ship and assault the bridge." The machine's voice mirrored the look on its face.

Ah ... so it is a bridge. And I guess this is actually my fault.

"I apologize for boarding your ship, but I wouldn't characterize it as an assault," Jason continued in a strong yet conciliatory tone. The robot stood with incredible speed and pointed to the access panel he had been working in.

"No? Then what the hell is that?! You ran onto the bridge and shot the nav sub-processor with that slug thrower of yours!" The level of emotion being displayed by the thing highly disturbed Jason for some reason. He lowered the rifle to the ground slowly and stood back up with his hands raised, palms down, in a placating gesture.

"Maybe we should start over. Who are you, and where am I?" More than anything, Jason wanted this question answered. After that, he would see if he could convince the machine to take him home. As Jason spoke, the robot's posture relaxed and it walked with a fluid gait toward him. It stopped a pace away and leaned into him. Jason noticed that it looked to be about six feet tall as it peered at him. Again, he was startled by how life-like the eyes were.

"Now see? Isn't that much more civilized than barging in and shooting up the bridge?" The being's sarcastic manner still had Jason out of sorts so he simply nodded. Once he did, the thing broke into a huge, closed-mouth smile. Jason maintained his gaze, locked onto its eyes, despite the overwhelming urge to see just what the hell the thing had in its mouth. Was there a tongue? Teeth? If so, why? It continued, striding away from him with its hands clasped behind its back as it walked, "My name is Deetz. This ship is a Jepsen Aero DL7 heavy gunship. It's something of a rarity now as Jepsen is no longer building ships. Or anything for that matter." Deetz glanced Jason's way at that last part. "It's not important. Anyway, she's small by most warship standards, but nearly indestructible. Gravimetric *and* thrust drives, plasma weapons and heavy particle beams as well as the normal complement of lasers, missiles, disruptors, and countermeasures one would expect." Jason arched an eyebrow at the term "indestructible" as he looked around the bridge. In addition to the bullet hole he personally had added, the bridge appeared to have suffered some damage and perhaps a fire recently.

"So you're a robot?" Jason had to get this out of the way. For some reason he couldn't get the scene from a popular sci-fi out of his head where a tiny alien was riding around in the head of a human-looking machine. At this question Deetz paused its pacing and cocked its head, considering the word.

"Since we don't really know each other, I'm going to assume you're not trying to be insulting. The term robot refers to a non-intelligent, programmable machine, not unlike the sort that likely built the superstructure of this ship. I am a synthetic life form, or synth if you prefer slang." Deetz turned from Jason and consulted a display of one of the terminals on the port side of the bridge.

"No offense intended. We have nothing so advanced on my ... world." Jason was still struggling with the concept of being in a space ship in orbit around ... "Where the hell are we? I remember seeing Saturn outside the canopy the first time I was up here."

"Ah, yes. Currently I'm trying to effect repairs and I needed raw materials to feed the fabricators to get some of the parts I'll need. Unfortunately, Saturn's rings are mostly water ice, not particularly helpful. So we're currently *en route* back to the rocky planets of this system. There looked to be some ruins of an advanced civilization on the fourth planet."

"Mars?!" Jason was stunned. "We weren't aware of anything there other than, well, dirt. Why not head to Earth? We have lots of raw material, I'd imagine."

Deetz rolled its eyes, "What do you think I was doing there in the first place? Your home is rife with refined metals, but your small attack aircraft pack quite a punch, which is why

I took off prematurely. You must have snuck aboard when I lowered the cargo bay ramp to exchange the atmosphere."

That explained the smoke coming out of the vents in the cargo bay when he'd first boarded. "So how is it I was able to sneak aboard and make it all the way to the bridge without detection? There has to be some sort of sensor system on board. Right?"

"Of course. This ship has an incredibly sophisticated anti-intrusion system that can detect and neutralize any threat that makes it on board." Deetz was again distractedly looking over displays. When he looked back Jason raised his arms, palms up, and shook his head in the universal 'So what the hell?' sign. "You may have noticed the decor," Deetz gestured to the scorch marks on the bulkheads. "There was a bit of a ... disagreement ... over who, exactly, owned the airspace we were flying in. They settled the argument with a high-energy plasma bolt as I was transitioning to slip-space. Many sub-systems are still down ship-wide." Jason ignored the flip between 'we' and 'I' during Deetz's narration, for the moment.

"What is slip-space? Is that like ..."

"While I would love to give a lecture on the miracles of modern star travel, I'm a bit pressed at the moment. With most of the automation knocked out, steering this thing safely by myself is a bit of a challenge." Deetz gestured to a seat in front of a terminal with darkened monitors, "Now if you wouldn't mind, have a seat, quietly, while I try to get a handle on this. I greatly appreciate it." Jason couldn't help but notice the strange flux in accents as it spoke English; most notable was the shift between American and UK inflections and dialect. It gave him an important clue as to how the ... *synth, was it?* ... had learned the Earth language. Being the most prevalent language in digital media, Jason assumed it must have assimilated it via broadcasts and probably the Internet.

While some dismissed him intellectually because of the line of work he chose and the lifestyle he lived, Jason Burke was no idiot. He knew Deetz was not telling him everything, although that in and of itself didn't concern him. After all, he was a stowaway from a comparatively primitive world. It was more a sense that the synth was *hiding* something. It had mentioned that the ship had been engaged in a battle recently. Was the crew killed, then? He had to assume a ship this large had a bigger complement than a single synthetic life form; the fact there was a galley that looked large enough to feed twenty people indicated that there were at least some biological beings on board at one time.

This reverie was interrupted by a drop in the pitch of what Jason assumed was the sound of the engines. He watched silently as Deetz strode across the bridge and looked at a display at one of the forward stations, then out through the canopy, and then back at the display again. He walked back to the station on the raised dais and started manipulating the controls. The stars tilted wildly outside the canopy and the engines came back up to power.

"So, what's up?" Jason couldn't stand being a chair decoration any longer.

"Just trying to get a bearing on Mars so I can get a good orbital insertion vector," Deetz said.

"Seems like this thing would have a more precise way to locate it," Jason stated, more out of an attempt to keep the conversation going.

"Oh, it does," Deetz was openly glaring at him. "But *someone* shot a hole in it." Jason fell silent and pretended to be fascinated by the trim on the terminal in front of him.

It was another thirty minutes or so, at least as near as Jason could tell, before Mars began to dominate the forward view. He couldn't believe how different it was to see the planet with his own eyes rather than through a telescope eyepiece or a digital image. It was with a pang of regret that he realized he didn't really get to appreciate the view of Saturn when he had the chance. Being debilitated by sheer terror and then getting hit with an anti-personnel weapon had kind of spoiled the whole thing.

As much as he was in awe of the view, the rate of closure on the planet was beginning to alarm him. Although he knew next to nothing about orbital mechanics, he had seen the film *Apollo 13* a few dozen times while deployed; at this rate of speed, there was no way they could safely enter the atmosphere or achieve a stable orbit. As his muscles tensed involuntarily and he gripped the armrests of his seat, his fears proved to be unfounded. Deetz further manipulated the controls and the ship decelerated abruptly, so quickly in fact that it seemed like they had simply stopped in space. Jason knew this sort of drastic negative acceleration should have put him through the forward canopy, and it was only then that he consciously realized that he was still firmly planted on the floor. Artificial gravity. It stood to reason that if whoever built this thing had the technology to keep him from floating out of his seat, then they also had the ability to null out the effects of inertia.

Though moving markedly slower, the ship was still moving at a few tens of thousands of miles per hour. Soon Deetz swung the ship from a head-on collision course with the red planet to a heading that would put them into a geosynchronous orbit over the equator. The synth rolled the ship so that Mars now hung above their heads in the canopy. It looked over to Jason and did a quick double brow raise that reminded him of Groucho Marx, along with a tight, closed-mouth grin. Again, the human was startled at how very human-like the alien machine's mannerisms were. He assumed it was for his benefit and he wasn't sure if he felt better knowing that or not. He looked up to notice Deetz was marching off the bridge.

"What's up?" Jason asked for the second time in the last twenty minutes.

"Sensor stations on the bridge are still down. I'm going to astral navigation to use the ship sensors to locate our landing site." The synth said this last part over its right shoulder, turning its head far more than a biological biped with a spine would be able to do. Jason hopped out of his seat and went to follow it. He paused at the AR-15 he had laid on the floor when he'd entered. While it was useless without ammo and seemingly unnecessary, the military part of his brain couldn't abide his weapon lying haphazardly on the deck. He picked it up, cleared it out of habit, and propped it up in one of the seats on the bridge after collapsing down the stock.

Shuffling quickly off the bridge, Jason found the synth in one of the side rooms off the starboard side of the passageway right outside the bridge entrance. The room was dominated by a large tabletop display that Deetz was hunched over; it didn't even look up as Jason entered the small room. Looking around, he saw the bulkheads were festooned with additional displays and control panels, most of which were in that strange written language that was found all throughout the ship that he couldn't hope to comprehend.

"What are we doing again?" He found long gaps in the conversation between the alien machine and himself to be unnerving.

"*We* are doing nothing. *I* am preparing to use the dorsal tactical sensor array to find a good landing spot. *You* are standing in my way as well as distracting me." Deetz gently nudged him out of the way as he manipulated the touch panel controls of the large tabletop display. "The terrain mapping sensor array is, of course, offline. The tactical array isn't really designed for this sort of thing, but it should be able to detect a large enough concentration of refined metals to indicate the location we want." An alert sound cut off the synth and multiple displays began streaming data that Jason couldn't read. He was watching Deetz as it frowned.

"Does your species have a presence on this planet?"

"No, we've only been as far as our own moon. Oh … wait, there are some robotic probes in orbit as well as a handful of landers and rovers on the surface. Nothing that poses any kind of threat, if that's what you're asking."

"Ah. That would explain why so many active satellites are completely ignoring us. Strictly exploratory then?" When Jason nodded it continued, "Very good. As primitive as your tech is, in our current shape a few of your concussive missiles could prove problematic." For some reason Jason still bristled at the casual insults the synth tossed out about humanity and its level of sophistication.

"So I thought you said this thing was indestructible. Seems something took a chunk out of its ass."

"I said it was *nearly* indestructible. It's one of the toughest gunships ever built; however, a direct hit by a plasma bolt from a frontline warship's main guns is a bit much for even it. Anything else in this class of ship would have been a cloud of ionized particles after a hit like that."

Jason was almost positive that he didn't want to know who had shot at the ship, or why. He hoped that after Deetz repaired the ship it would take him back to Earth, preferably to the same place it had picked him up from. However, he did have to admit that the thrill of the situation was intoxicating. Alien gunships involved in deep space combat; ruins of an ancient civilization on Mars; a walking, talking machine that claimed to be a life form … it was all so much to process that Jason's mind ignored the fantastic aspects of it and focused on what he could understand. It was also exhausting. He had been running on a constant adrenaline rush since he had spotted the ship streaking though the night sky, excluding the times he had been knocked unconscious, and it was beginning to catch up with him. He stood in the doorway of the room to give Deetz the space he needed to work and he was beginning to have trouble keeping his eyes open. This didn't go unnoticed by the synth.

"You should get some sleep. You've been stressed and injured. You're going to fall out where you stand if you don't get some rest. We're not going to make landfall for some hours yet; you can sleep in one of the crew staterooms. Follow me." Deetz brushed past Jason and headed down the corridor towards the flight of stairs and the large common area. The exhausted human stumbled after him while some part of his tired brain again wondered where the rest of the crew for the ship was. The synth led him around to the port side of ship along the outer bulkhead of the common area and into a short side corridor. It stopped before an interior hatch and pressed the control panel that was situated to the right of the door. It slid open to revel a sparse but comfortable-looking stateroom.

Walking into the room, Jason could see that whoever designed the ship must have had similar physiology as himself: the bed, chair, even the very room looked strikingly similar to rooms he had seen aboard U.S. Navy warships. That was yet one more thing he wanted to ask Deetz about, but for right now the only thing he could think about was the bed.

"I'll just lay down for a couple hours, I'll be good to go after that."

"Of course. Take however long your species needs to recover from your ordeal. I'll be on the bridge." Deetz turned and walked out, the door closing automatically behind him. Jason sat on the bed and pondered the strange being for a moment. In addition to swinging between regional dialects of Earth, its personality also seemed to shift between a snarky, biting sarcasm to the very soul of courtesy. He again felt that nagging suspicion that something terrible had befallen the crew of this ship, and that he should be careful how much he trusted the strange being that had walked out of the room moments ago. But, for the moment, nothing seemed more important than getting some sleep. With the multiple instances of unconsciousness, one caused by blunt force trauma, he really had no sense of how long he had actually been on the ship. He was asleep before his head had fully compressed the pillow.

Chapter 4

In a nice change of pace, Jason awoke naturally, in a comfortable bed, and not terrified, injured, or both. He yawned and stretched as if he had awoken in the bed in his cabin, which was a little over fifteen million miles away at that instant. He swung his legs around the bed and stood up, noticed he had left his boots on when he fell asleep, and made his way out the door after smacking the control on the bulkhead. After a couple of steps he knew something had changed, and this time he knew what it was: the gravity was different again. Unlike when he'd first made his way on board, however, this was a very pronounced change. He took an exploratory leap in the corridor and felt like he glided all the way into the large common area at the heart of the ship. Deetz must be messing with the artificial gravity again.

Once the novelty of the reduced gravity had run its course, he also noticed the change in smell. While it still had that distinct "aircraft smell," a unique mixture of lubricants, alloys, and fuels, there was also a strong chemical cleaner smell riding over top of that. He walked out further into the main area and jerked his head around as some small, squat machines zipped across the area and out of his field of view.

"*Those* are robots," Deetz said with a lopsided grin as it made its way down the stairs, apparently coming from the bridge. "They're part of the ship's damage control system. They'll scurry around and continually repair and clean things. They'll polish holes through the deck plating if you don't order them into inactivity once in a while." Deetz gave an odd chuckle at his own joke. "In actuality, they're always underfoot if you just allow them to run wild. Their big brothers are at work outside on the hull and there are some more specialized models that are doing system level repairs."

"Hmm." Jason was noncommittal. The synth had shown yet another side to itself; now it was the charming host.

"You must be hungry. The bio analysis the med-bay performed when you were ... subdued ... indicated that your species' metabolism requires a fairly regular intake of food."

What in the hell is this thing up to. I feel like I'm being set up for something.

"Yeah. To be honest, I'm starving." At his response Deetz's head snapped up and his face assumed an alarmed expression.

"You're starving?! Why did you not make me aware of this earlier?" Deetz rushed over and grabbed Jason by the wrist and began to lead him aft towards what he had earlier assumed was the galley. The human's protests did little against the incredible casual strength of the synth. Deetz was practically dragging Jason like he was a toddler.

"Deetz! It's a figure of speech, I'm not actually starving. I'm just really, really hungry. Seriously! Fucking let me go!" The light gravity did little to help Jason's ability to catch himself after Deetz released him, so he stumbled and sprawled out on the floor face down in an undignified heap. He let out a weary sigh.

"Are you okay, Jason?" This was the first time the artificial being had used his name, another red flag in Jason's naturally suspicious mind.

"Nothing hurt but my pride," he replied glibly as he bounced back up with a move that only light gravity would allow. "Now. About that food ..."

"Of course. This way." The synth now assumed the mannerisms of a maître d' as it gestured towards the galley with a subdued, but still present flourish. Jason gave it an odd look as he walked by and realized that despite the very human mannerisms the machine exhibited, it was still an alien. It had accessed and compiled Earth's media into a completely disjointed set of responses to Jason's actions. There was no doubt about its intelligence, but its motives were both a mystery and a concern. He walked across the common area and made his way to the galley. At Deetz's gesture he sat at the long, high-top-style table that looked like it could seat at least ten people. There was another identical table across from him that led him to believe that the ship's intended complement must be between fifteen to twenty-five people ... er, beings.

"The ship's computer was able to devise a safe menu for you from the initial bio scans that were taken when you were injured. While it certainly won't be an Earth meal, it won't make you sick either." Deetz had walked back behind a counter into the food prep area and began stabbing at another of the ship's touchscreen displays that was mounted in the wall. After a few moments, he walked back around with a tray that held a steaming plate and a tall glass of water. Jason had been too distracted to see where the food had come from so quickly. "Here we are," Deetz said cheerfully as he set the tray in front of Jason. While it looked odd, it did smell good. Some sort of white meat/protein and a green vegetable that he couldn't identify. At least the water was still water. He dug in with gusto and was relieved to find that, big surprise, it tasted similar to chicken. While he ate, Deetz sat across from him, propped his elbows on the table and steepled his fingers, fixing him with a steady stare. It was a tad unnerving while he was trying to eat, but he was too hungry to care or pause long enough to tell the synth to stop staring.

"So ... you were a soldier on Earth?" The question caught Jason off guard.

"Technically I was an airman. But yes, I did serve in the military." Jason didn't volunteer any further information. He sensed he was treading on delicate ground right now.

"I suppose there's a distinction there I'm missing, but you were a warrior among your people?"

"Yes."

"There's no need for such discomfort, Jason Burke," Deetz said with that alarming mechanical laugh. "This is not an interrogation. I'm just curious about what type of human you are. Would anyone of your species have boarded a strange ship brandishing a weapon?"

"No. I suppose I'm a special case, even among the warriors on Earth." Jason relaxed a bit, but not much. "To be honest, I didn't realize just *how* strange this ship was when I first saw it. It looked like it could have possibly been something conceived and built on Earth, at least from the outside. It wasn't until I saw the language on the bulkheads, and saw you on the bridge, that I realized what I was actually on. My original intent had been to render aid."

"Render aid?" Deetz repeated with a frown. "But you brought no medical supplies, only a fairly powerful weapon." This caused Jason to pause in his eating and shift uncomfortably.

"There's a reason I live a remote, solitary life right now. I fought extensively in a few of our wars, and I feel better being well-armed when approaching the unknown. It may be paranoia, but then again, maybe not." He looked pointedly at the synth as he said the last sentence. Deetz chose to ignore the challenge.

"What some would deem as paranoia others would see as prudence. So your planet is currently under invasion? I didn't detect any traces of other ships on my approach, but with the system damage that isn't saying that they weren't there."

"No, no. Nothing like that. We fight amongst ourselves over political and theological differences." As Jason said these words to an alien being he realized how truly foolish humanity must seem to an outsider. Not that he saw his world in such overly simplistic strokes, but when distilled down to its base components it did seem that there had to be a better way than slaughtering each other.

"You say that as if you're apologizing on behalf of your species. There's nothing unusual about your planet's history. Evolution is a violent struggle in which only the strongest and most fierce reach the pinnacle to become a world's dominant species. Many species don't survive their own instincts and destroy themselves before they ever realize they're part of a much larger interstellar community." Deetz pushed back from the table and rose as he finished speaking. "Go ahead and finish your meal. You can meet me on the bridge after you're done."

Jason slowly chewed his food as he considered the synth's words. So if every species that survived to dominate their own world shared that fighting spirit, the idea of the benevolent extraterrestrials coming to Earth and ushering in a new era of peace and prosperity for humanity seemed unlikely. He mentally shrugged; Earth was nowhere near being able to reach out beyond its own star system so it was more of a "what if" fantasy than a real concern.

He polished off that delightful whatever-the-hell-it-was with the glass of water and felt much better. When he looked around for someplace to put the dishes, one of the small squat robots darted out from behind the counter, snatched the tray from his hands, and hauled ass back around the counter. "What the shit!?" he said aloud. *Was that thing watching me eat the whole time? Creepy.* He walked out of the galley and up towards the bridge, still contemplating the new world he found himself in and how humanity would ever fit into it. Assuming it even survived that long.

His arrival to the bridge was greeted with yet another surprise. They had already landed sometime while he was asleep. Jason had watched countless Space Shuttle landings on television and the re-entry process looked quite rough, but somehow he had slept through the entire thing. He saw that they were parked at the edge of an unfathomably large ravine. *Valles Marineris?* Jason was also startled at the change on the bridge. The walls were gleaming and clean, the pall of burnt electrical components was gone, and the displays that ringed the command deck were all lit cheerfully.

"Looks like you've got everything up and running," he said as a way of announcing his presence. The last time he'd surprised the synth he took a nasty shot from *something*.

"We're in much better shape than we were, that's for certain. Some of the major systems are still being repaired but the hull is one hundred percent and the main computer is back up and talking to the individual subsystems. Most importantly, the slip-drive will be back up soon." Deetz stood near the canopy on the starboard side of the bridge, appearing to look down into the trench.

"Something interesting?"

"Not particularly. Just watching the bots drag up raw material. We couldn't safely land any closer to the structure they're dismantling and bringing back up to feed into the fabricators, so the process is taking longer than it should." Deetz turned towards him, appearing pensive.

"Fabricator?"

"Machines that are part of the damage control system. You can feed them raw material and they will rearrange the molecular structure and produce completed parts needed for repairs. It's almost unheard of on a ship this small, but the smaller versions we have on board are invaluable."

"So there's the ruins of an ancient Martian civilization down there?" Jason's voice had a hint of awe in it.

"Indeed. It appears that the structure embedded in the walls of this trench was some sort of emergency shelter. So with all the probes crawling and flying over this planet you haven't detected any signs of the life that was here before the atmosphere bled off?" Deetz's question seemed more an effort at idle conversation than a genuine curiosity.

"Nope. But our sensor capability is far less than what you have here." Jason could sense there was something Deetz was wanting to ask him, and considering how accommodating it had been since he woke up he assumed that it needed help with something. He didn't have to wait long for confirmation of this.

"So I have a proposition for you, Jason." *And here comes the pitch.* "How anxious are you to get back to Earth?" *Is this thing fucking kidding me?*

"Well, Deetz, I'd have to say the sooner the better. For both of us I'd imagine."

"Maybe not." The synth clasped its hands behind its back and started pacing along the forward edge of the ship's canopy. "There may be a way we can help each other. As you may have noticed, I'm currently short a crew. I won't go into the details about where they might be as it is not germane to the topic. What is, however, is the fact that we were in the middle of a job that, at this juncture, requires a biological." Deetz paused his pacing and turned to fix Jason with a stare. When the human didn't respond other than to cross his arms over his chest, the synth continued, "As shocking as it may seem, there are some backwards planets that don't recognize the rights of synthetics. In other words, I am little more than an animated curiosity to these people. But as a biological, you would be able to operate freely at these places."

"That's all very light in details, Deetz. What, exactly, am I supposed to be doing?"

"It couldn't be simpler. We have some cargo that had an extended delivery date. We stored it on a safe world so we could free up our cargo bay with the intention of retrieving it later. But with the aforementioned prejudices, I cannot secure the release of the cargo from those who are currently holding it for us." The synth's humanistic mannerisms had been dropped; a blank machine stared back at Jason. *Damn, don't ever play poker with this thing.*

"So the only reason you need me is because this place doesn't recognize you as a … person. Why would they give a shit about me?"

"The ship's transponder is the only proof of signature required. Once we land, the cargo will be released to any member of the crew automatically. All I have to do is add you to the manifest." The sincerity Deetz managed to put into that blank expression was admirable. Jason still didn't trust it, and moreover, had no reason to want to help it. He had boarded this ship in good faith believing he was responding to an aviation mishap; moonlighting as an interstellar FedEx man wasn't in the cards for him. But … it would be a hell of an adventure. Since boarding the ship he had felt himself coming alive again in a way that he hadn't experienced since before the wars. Not that he was a combat junkie, but the highs and lows during that part of his life were *so* high and *so* low that he only felt a numbness inside since he had come home. As tempting as it was, however, his sense of self-preservation was still strong, and he still *knew* this thing was lying to him on some level.

"Do I have to decide right now?"

"No. We are still some hours away from being ready to launch. You should take some time to consider everything. I understand it's a lot to take in. Perhaps a walk would do you some good."

"A walk? Where? Around the cargo bay?"

"If you wish. But *there*," Deetz said, nodding towards the view outside the canopy, "would probably be a bit more interesting for you." The little boy inside Jason that had wanted to be an astronaut started jumping up and down.

"Seriously?"

"Of course. Your bipedal configuration is fairly common. We have environmental suits on board that would easily fit you. Interested?" Deetz, as did any good salesman, seemed to sense he had Jason hooked. Now he just had to reel him in.

"Oh, hell yeah, I'm interested. Let's do this." Jason followed Deetz off the bridge at a quick clip. "So why did you turn the gravity down some more?"

"I didn't. This is Mars-normal. I had to turn all the grav generators off when repairs to the slip-drive reactor started, that includes deck plating."

"There was reactor damage?" Jason was alarmed by this, having only a vague working knowledge of nuclear fission reactors used on Earth.

"Yes. Not to worry, though. The slip-drive reactor is well established technology. When it goes offline the binary fuel can be harmlessly shunted overboard so the pressures don't reach critical levels." The nonchalant manner of Deetz's explanation set Jason's mind at ease. Somewhat.

Chapter 5

The environmental suit wasn't exactly what Jason was imagining. While he was picturing the bulky space suits like the NASA astronauts used, the system he wore was no more cumbersome than a jogging suit. The first layer of the suit was custom-made by the computer in a few minutes to fit skintight over his body. This was the pressure layer; the active material could maintain the correct pressure against his skin so that a pressurized environment wouldn't be necessary within the suit. The outer layer was a tougher, thicker material that controlled his body temperature and protected against punctures. Finally, there was a sort of hard-shell vest that controlled all suit functions, handled communications, and housed the re-breather apparatus. Once Deetz had programmed the unit for an Earth-like oxygen/nitrogen mixture, Jason was nearly ready. The last step had been for the synth to program the helmet to display English on the heads-up display so Jason would be able to understand the warnings and status indicators. The helmet itself was also unlike the familiar NASA equipment; instead of a large, pressurized "bell" in which a person could move their head about, this was more like a fitted motorsports helmet with an oversized visor. Getting fitted and decked out in the gear had taken less than thirty minutes.

A few minutes after walking back into the corridor, carrying his helmet under his right arm like any other Earth-born astronaut, Jason was once again entering the main cargo hold. Before he could even think about donning his helmet, Deetz walked over and began punching controls on the touchscreen panel that was mounted in the pedestal next to the main rear doors. A loud alarm started up a cadence and red strobes began flashing on either side of the doors as they slid apart, revealing the cargo ramp still up in the locked position. But, to Jason's horror, it also began to move as it jerked and then lowered smoothly away, revealing the barren Martian landscape.

"Shit!" Jason shouted as he clumsily tried to jam the helmet onto his head in a panic. After two attempts, he still couldn't get the locking collar that sealed to the outer layer to go over his head.

"What is your problem? I thought you wanted to go out there," Deetz's calm voice floated across the cargo bay to him. Jason then realized that not only had there been no explosive decompression, but he could hear the other's voice so there had to still be atmosphere in the bay. That and he was still hyperventilating. He pulled the helmet back off and lowered it slowly, trying to salvage as much of his dignity as he could.

"So I take it there's something keeping the air inside?"

"Obviously. There's an electrostatic shield keeping the atmosphere in, though it won't do anything to stop solid objects from coming in or out." Deetz walked back to the middle of the bay where Jason still stood and took the helmet from his hands. It flipped it around and helped him slide it easily down over his head. After verifying the seals and ensuring the re-breather was attached and functioning, he slapped Jason on top of the helmet and pointed outside the bay. "Have fun. You can call back to me if you have any trouble. Just stay out of the way of the bots that are shuttling up material from the trench. They're not very smart or attentive. You don't want one to smack into you." With that, it turned and walked back up the stairs and disappeared back into the ship through the hatch, leaving Jason standing alone in the cargo hold.

Passing through the shield that was holding in the cargo hold's atmosphere was fairly anticlimactic; he couldn't tell any difference at all, save for the display in his helmet alerting him of the external pressure change. The suit took up the slack seamlessly and he soon found himself standing with the toes of both boots right at the edge of the cargo ramp. He couldn't help but feel a chill run up his spine as he was about to leapfrog over decades of human technological development (and astronaut screening) to become the first human to walk on Mars. He felt he should say something inspirational, but his mind was so numbed from recent events he just stared blankly down at the reddish-brown dirt in front of him. *Fuck it. Inspirational isn't really my style anyway.* He picked his right foot up, let himself drop down, and put a boot print in the soil. Despite himself, he could feel his eyes well up with tears as the enormity of what he had just done hit him.

The lighter gravity of Mars made locomotion a bit of a challenge at first. He tried to do the hop-skip thing like Buzz Aldrin had done on Earth's moon, but the gravity was *too* strong for that. He eventually found that if he moved with a normal gait but pushed off with his toes at the very end he would drift a good distance for not a lot of effort spent. He looked back at the ship and noticed a few squat, multi-appendage robots dragging what looked to be chunks of slag metal under the ship and lifting them up into an iris-type opening that was forward and port of the main cargo hold. He surmised that it must be the input to the fabricators. Turning his back on the ship and all the repair activity, Jason set off along the perimeter of Valles Marineris, marveling at its enormity. He had been to the Grand Canyon back on Earth a couple of times, but this was something else entirely. It was almost like the world stopped right before him. After what felt like a couple of kilometers, he came up to a small outcropping and stopped. He stared out over the canyon for a few minutes, then sat down cross-legged in the Martian dirt and looked out while his thoughts turned inward. The place looked like northern Iraq after a haboob blew through; it even had the same reddish hue from the weak light filtering through the dust.

Jason stared out, unseeing, as his thoughts flitted around in his head. He was a person who was naturally able to compartmentalize during situations of extreme stress—it was how he was able to operate so successfully during the war. However, he was starting to fully realize what it was that he had stumbled into, and he suddenly felt very, very small.

Not only had he inadvertently gotten himself shanghaied aboard an alien spacecraft, but now the sole occupant (a smart-assed alien machine) wanted to take him along on a job of some sort. What could the ramifications of this be? What if something unforeseen happened and, as Earth's unofficial, unsanctioned ambassador to the stars, his world was made to suffer the consequences for his actions? His thoughts drifted to the beautiful blonde in the picture he carried; what would happen to her? He quickly shoved the entire line of reasoning from his head lest he rip open that wound again. While she was never far from his mind, he had learned to keep those memories buried, if only just under the surface.

Even as he went through the mental tedium of trying to talk himself out of going along with Deetz on this mission, he knew what his answer would be in the end. In spite of everything, the adventure was simply too much for him to pass up. That same lust for excitement that made him enlist in the Air Force at eighteen was also pushing him to climb aboard the gunship and blast off for the stars.

"Jason, can you hear me?"

Speaking of the devil …

"Yes Deetz, I copy. What can I do for you? Over."

"Over what?"

"Never mind," Jason rolled his eyes. "What do you need?"

"Just curious about how much longer you'll be. We're about done with repairs and will be ready for lift in approximately an hour."

"Already? That was fast."

"Not especially so. You've been out there for a few hours now."

Jason rose easily to his feet, looking like a gymnast in the light Martian gravity. "I'm on the bounce. I'll be back shortly." On the bounce ... he laughed at the irony of using a line from one of his favorite novels as he actually bounced across an alien planet in a spacesuit. If only Heinlein could see him.

Approaching the gunship, Jason could see significant changes, most notably to the hull which had been splotchy with burn marks and scarred by blast impacts. It was now smooth and shone dully in the light like burnished steel. The cargo ramp was still down so Jason bounced up and into the hold, stumbling slightly as the gravity doubled. It appeared that artificial gravity had been restored, so Jason had to assume the slip-drive reactor was also up and running without incident. After popping the seal on his helmet and removing it, Jason could *really* feel what the damage control system had done. The ship positively hummed with energy: a low-frequency, omnipresent tingle that hadn't been there before. As he made his way across the cargo bay, Deetz's voice came over the ship's public address system.

"Meet me in the room you suited up in and I'll help you out of that thing. We should be ready to get out of here once you're dressed again."

It was at least forty minutes after boarding before Jason was free of the exo-atmospheric suit. "These things aren't really designed to be quick or convenient. Nearly anyone who would serve aboard a ship like this would have a much more capable combat suit that they would wear. These are more contingency items." This last comment brought Jason's thoughts right back to the missing crew, and the synth's evasiveness about where they might be. He decided to ignore the thought that was nagging at the back of his mind, as he had more or less decided to go with Deetz on this cargo run. Dwelling on it wouldn't do him any good.

As he laced up his boots while sitting on a bench, he asked Deetz a question, "So how long of a flight is it to this cargo pickup?" Silence. Looking around, he noticed he was talking to himself as the synth was nowhere in the room. "Well what the hell?" He couldn't believe Deetz had been able to so easily exit the room without his noticing. Either his situational awareness wasn't nearly as good as he had been led to believe, or the synth was extremely sneaky. Shrugging, he stood up and stretched, enjoying the normal gravity, and strode out of the room on his way to the bridge.

Walking onto the bridge, Jason was further impressed at how alive the ship seemed now. Deetz stood in the middle of the raised dais in the center, feet shoulder width apart and hands on its hips. Jason had already become accustomed to the human-like gestures and mannerisms the machine exhibited, so its appearance no longer startled him. "So, what's the play?"

"I'd say that depends on what your decision is. So, what will it be? Ready for the adventure of a lifetime?" The cheesy, used car salesman act Deetz was doing grated on Jason's nerves.

"Yes. I'm going with you," Jason began, ignoring the wide smile that appeared on the synth's face. "But, I want it made clear that I'm simply a glorified passenger. I'm trusting that you aren't planning on tossing me into anything more … involved … than just being a biological at the pickup." Jason realized how idiotic his speech was. He would be a de facto prisoner once they were there, marooned God knows how many light years from Earth. If Deetz had nefarious intentions, Jason would be in no position to do anything about it. Still, the risk-to-reward ratio was still tipping the scale in favor of going along for the ride.

"Not an issue. You'll just disembark, tag a couple forms, and we'll be on our way. You'll get to see some incredible things before I bring you back to your planet."

"Okay. We ready to rock then? I'm assuming this bird is at one hundred percent." Jason especially appreciated the clean processed air that the environmental system was pumping out. It was a vast improvement over the acrid aroma of burnt electronics and ozone.

"Oh, not quite at one hundred percent; the damage control system is good, but it can't work miracles. There are some things that will require some better equipped facilities to get back to full strength." Deetz was settling into the left hand seat on the dais and motioned to the seat at his right for Jason to sit in. As soon as he sat in the seat, it began to subtly adjust itself to his body shape. It gave in the right places and bolstered in the others; the result was one of the most comfortable seats he had ever sat in. It gave the initial impression of suede leather, but upon further inspection, was definitely some sort of synthetic material.

Jason looked bemusedly at the array of controls and displays before him. It was an interesting mix of familiar toggle and tactile switches along with the more expected glass touch panels and, he noticed with delight, a pair of holographic displays. One of them showed the ship in its entirety, slowly rotating, with key information being displayed with arrows indicating parts of the model. The other seemed to show the Solar System with Mars clearly highlighted by a rotating halo. On a whim, he closed two fingers and his thumb together and pushed his hand towards the Mars icon in the model. Once he felt like he was "touching" it, he quickly splayed the three digits outward. The result was satisfyingly as he expected: the holo zoomed quickly until it was showing only a rotating Mars in exquisite detail along with more scrolling text. There was also a red strobing crosshair flashing near the Valles Marineris that he knew must indicate their position. He assumed if he "swiped" again that the holo would zoom in even further and maybe even show the ship itself. Instead, he inserted his open hand into the holo and quickly closed all his fingers together, zooming the display back out to the original display of the Solar System. The interface was eerily intuitive for the human to operate and said a lot about the beings who'd designed and built the system. "If you're done playing ..."

Jason looked over at Deetz sheepishly. "Just playing a hunch," he said.

"Ah. Well, if you're done we can lift off and get out of here. Once we're in flight, please try to control your hunches; I'd rather not have one of them activate the self-destruct." Deetz's hands flew over the controls and a deep, steady hum started building in volume and pitch.

"This thing actually has a self-destruct?"

"No."

Deetz rested his hands on two dimly glowing hemispheres on either side of his seat, the blue light shining weakly between his fingers. While Jason couldn't exactly make out the motions the synth made, it was obvious these were the manual flight controls when the ground dropped away. He quickly gave up trying to decipher how the controls actually worked, being a far cry from the familiar stick and rudder, and enjoyed the view as Mars slid underneath them at an increasingly fast rate. Deetz was speaking out loud in that same alien dialect he'd used when Jason first stormed the bridge, obviously talking to the ship. As he spoke, Jason could hear and feel changes in its configuration; some solid thumps seemed to be the landing gear coming up and locking and the pitch of that oppressive whine seemed to be directly related to their speed. "Want to see something incredible?" Deetz was now looking over at him.

How does one say no to that? "Of course," he said. He would come to regret those words immensely. Deetz sharply spoke out a single word. The lights on the bridge dimmed instantly and a whole new set of displays came up in front of Jason. Before he could ask if the lighting change was the incredible thing he was waiting for, a hearty *BOOM* resounded from somewhere aft of the bridge and the ship leapt forward with enough ferocity to press him back in the seat despite the artificial gravity. Deetz made a series of exaggerated motions with the controls and the ship swung wildly until it was pointing nose down and plunging back towards the Martian surface. He leveled out a split second before Jason would have screamed in alarm, but there would be plenty of time for that later. They shot over the edge of the Valles Marineris trench and banked hard to the right while descending into the enormous chasm. Despite the fact that the Martian geological feature dwarfed the Grand Canyon on Earth, the speed at which the ship was rocketing into it made it seem no larger than a drainage ditch. The canyon walls rose up until they completely blocked the view of the sky through the canopy, and Deetz was still accelerating and *still* in a dive, heading for the bottom.

For the second time in as many minutes, the ship leveled out deep within the trench just as Jason's muscles clenched up and an alarmed yelp would have escaped his lips. The velocity at which they were powering up the canyon was stunning. Jason wished he could understand the scrolling numbers and indicators in front of him so he could know just *how* fast they were moving. Apparently that wasn't the extent of the incredible something that Deetz had promised. At another spoken command from the synth and a few hand movements on the controls, an immense roar issued forth from the engines and Jason was planted hard back into his seat. The ship's speed increased to what could only be described as suicidal as they thundered along the floor of the canyon, kicking up a huge trailing plume of dust. Deetz had a wide, maniacal smile on his metallic face as he piloted the ship in a terrain-hugging course that brought them perilously close to the rises along either side. Jason had gotten an "incentive ride" in an F-16 fighter jet during his time in the service, but it didn't compare to the thrill/terror of blasting along the alien landscape in an equally alien, and incredibly powerful, spaceship.

After ninety seconds of the wild ride had elapsed, Deetz yanked the ship into a vertical climb that pressed Jason back into his seat even more. Now staring straight up into the Martian sky, he watched with wonder as they transitioned from flying in the atmosphere into space. The majesty of the moment was juxtaposed with the roar of the engines as the ship clawed its way up Mars' gravity well. Deetz barked another command in that alien language and the vibration, pull of acceleration, and engine roar all ceased. The ship felt like it was parked on the ground as they continued to pull away from Mars in a direct route away from the planet. Jason was completely ignorant of the science of putting a ship into orbit from a planet surface, but he knew enough to realize the power of the engines must be tremendous to be able to just pull up and away from a planet the way they had.

"I like to tweak down the inertial compensators and engine dampeners when I do that. It makes it so much more intense." Deetz's manic actions were replaced with the more familiar smooth and polished demeanor. Jason was forced to yet again re-evaluate how he viewed the synthetic life form; it was obvious it was able to experience a wide range of complex emotions, including not being above a little thrill seeking. He would need to keep this in mind. So far the synth was being cordial because it needed him, but that could change quickly.

As his vitals came back down to a normal level after the adrenaline rush Deetz's canyon blast had provided, Jason stared through the canopy at the stars. There seemed to be so many now that he was no longer separated from them by an atmosphere and the light pollution of modern civilization. It was quite peaceful really, as long as he didn't dwell on the reality of the situation he was in. But, now that he had made the decision to fly with Deetz on this new adventure, he felt the fear and trepidation slip away and he became anxious to see what was out there.

"Are we in ... slip-space?" If they were, Jason was sorely disappointed.

"No. The slip-drive emitters are being charged from the reactor. It will take a bit since the reactor was completely shut down during the repairs. It's a minor inconvenience. We have a few hours before we can activate the drive, was there anything else in this star system you've been dying to see?"

Jason thought hard about his answer. He'd already been up close and personal with Saturn and walked on Mars during his short time on board. What else did he want to see?

"I suppose I'd like to see Jupiter if we're heading that way." Being put on the spot like that, it was the only other interesting thing in the Solar System Jason could think of. He watched as Deetz punched some commands in on a control panel and sat back in its seat. There was no discernible difference in the ship save for a slight tick up in the pitch of the engines.

"On our way. Should be about ninety minutes if you'd like to grab something to eat." At Deetz's casual comment, Jason found he was suddenly famished. He felt tired as well, but he could tough it out for a bit longer. He rose from his seat and walked off the bridge. When he turned in the corridor he saw the synth had not come with him. He hoped the galley interface was as intuitive as the holo display on the bridge. Walking down the stairs (*Would it be called a ladder since it's on a ship?*), he strode purposefully into the galley area. As he'd expected, the lights came up and the panels lit in reaction to his proximity, and that was it. He stood looking at the foreign script in utter confusion, afraid to touch anything. After ninety seconds or so, the ship apparently tired of waiting for him.

"*Gaanantz shoowt.*" The disembodied voice, a pleasant sounding tenor, seemed as if it had come from the walls of the galley.

What the hell does that mean? "Um, I don't speak whatever language that is," Jason said to the wall.

There were a couple of beeps and then: "Earth dialect. English, United States. Would you like all ship functions in this language?"

"Uh, yeah! That'd be great." Jason assumed it simply meant would he like it to speak English to him, but then he noticed the touch panel displays all blinked off and when they came back on they were in good ol' English instead of the hopeless looking alien script.

"What are you doing down there?!" Deetz's shout came through on the intercom.

"I'm trying to get something to eat. Isn't that what it told me to do?"

"Every display up here is now in English!"

"The computer asked if I would like all functions in English. I didn't know it meant everywhere."

"Even the ship is a bigot," Deetz muttered, still being broadcast over the intercom. "Please tell it that only non-essential displays that YOU'RE using are to be in English, everything else is to be Jenovian Standard." Jason heard the intercom cut off so he didn't bother responding to Deetz. He directed his voice to one of the displays instead.

"You get that computer?" Silence. "Computer?"

"Standing by. Please state command."

"Please restore all essential functions to Jenovian Standard and display English only on displays that I am personally using." Jason hoped there wasn't a specific command syntax he was supposed to use.

"Acknowledged."

"*THANK YOU,*" came the sarcastic shout from the direction of the bridge. The smartass machine didn't even bother to use the ship's intercom that time. Rolling his eyes, Jason addressed the ship again.

"Could I get the same thing to eat I had earlier?" He wasn't brave enough to risk culinary variety just then.

"Acknowledged," the ship replied amiably. After a few moments there was a double beep and a panel slid up to allow a tray loaded with the familiar food to be pushed onto the serving counter. It was just like the chow hall, minus the surly staff. Jason took his tray over to one of the tables and wolfed down his food, barely tasting it as he ate with the mechanical efficiency that seemed to be a trait many military veterans shared. Afterwards he rose, drained the rest of the water in his glass, and hurried back towards the bridge, not bothering to wait and see if his tray would be collected again by one of the maintenance robots.

Chapter 6

Once back on the bridge, Jason walked past the command consoles and up as close as he could get to the steeply raked forward canopy without ducking. The view was breathtaking. The transparent material, which he assumed was something far more exotic than glass or Lexan, rose up over and well behind his head. The effect was like standing on a platform out in the middle of space; the sensation nearly gave him vertigo as he looked out at the stars. After a moment he realized one of the stars was becoming brighter and moving quickly across his field of view relative to the others. It could only be Jupiter. Jason couldn't even hope to calculate their speed, but judging by the rate that Jupiter's brightness was increasing it must be unimaginable by Earth-technology standards.

The furthest human from Earth stood transfixed as Jupiter began to resolve from a white speck into glorious detail. The synth sat silently in the command seat, ostensibly controlling the ship, but Jason could almost feel the eyes on him. He couldn't tell if Deetz was still feeling peevish about the language switch he had inadvertently caused on the displays or if it was something else that was keeping the normally over-talkative being quiet. Whatever the reason, Jason was grateful for it. He didn't want the moment ruined by a stream of inane chatter. The gas giant was swelling in his field of vision and he could make out the stripes of its atmosphere in exquisite detail. While he had viewed more than a few high-res photos taken by NASA's exploratory spacecraft, there was simply no comparison to gazing upon it with the naked eye. He felt the heady rush of discovery that had driven humans out of their comfort zones and into the unknown since man had discovered fire.

As he stared, sparks began to dance across the canopy. When he looked closer he could see that they were actually a foot or so in front of the transparent material. He looked back to Deetz questioningly.

"High energy particles coming off the planet. A gas giant like this puts off some serious radiation. If they're concentrated and intense enough, they interact with the collision shields." The synth hadn't had to look up to answer his unasked question; it had indeed been watching him. Although it could just be a continued curiosity, Jason couldn't shrug off the nagging distrust he had for the alien.

The gunship had by now swung into a high orbit over the system's largest planet. Deetz allowed the ship to adjust its velocity to achieve a stable orbit before bringing the nose around so that it was pointing directly at the planet and then slightly "down" towards the southern pole. This allowed for the largest viewing area through the forward canopy.

"I'm going to go check on some things in the engineering bays. We'll be here for a couple of hours, so enjoy." With that, Deetz hopped out from behind the command console and strode off the bridge, leaving Jason alone with Jupiter. He watched the synth exit in the faint reflection on the forward canopy. He turned back to the massive planet in front of him and simply enjoyed the moment; he was the first human to ever see this, and likely to be the only one for quite some time. The thought awed and humbled him. The vision of majestic Jupiter hanging so close it looked like he could touch it welled up his eyes with tears once again and cleared his mind of all doubt, fear, and regret, all of which he'd been feeling in spades since boarding the ship. No matter what happened from that moment on, Jason felt it would be worth this single moment in time, and it was something that could never be taken away from him.

Drifting over to the bench seat that ran along the front of the raised command stations, he seated himself into a comfortable slouch and addressed the ship, "Dim all ambient light on the bridge, please." The ship instantly obeyed by bringing down all the bridge lights and even the station displays until he was only illuminated by the light of the sun reflecting off the gas giant. The effect was breathtaking; it was like he was floating in space while looking at the planet.

There was so much to process. Given that, Jason felt he should be a lot more concerned or agitated than he was. Besides actually being on board the gunship, he felt like he was being bombarded and each new revelation had numbed his emotions to the point that he was simply observing these astounding events rather than reacting to them. It was his nature: things happened to him and he'd react later. It was somewhat off-putting to some; they felt he was cold or uncaring, but the truth was he simply couldn't generate an emotional response to traumatic events until he'd had time to really let it sink in. Then it would come all at once, often accompanied by the guilt of having been so distant while those around needed him the most. He'd like to be able to blame this on the war, or the military in general, but he'd always been like this. Often it had pushed people away from him. Just as his thoughts were beginning to turn back to "her," Deetz strode back in and startled him out of his reverie.

"Get your fill? We're all set. The reactor is still stuck in some sort of low-output mode, but the field emitters are fully charged and ready so we can enter slip-space. We're still going to have to use the main engines in normal space though." Deetz gracefully swung its mechanical body into the command seat and looked over to Jason expectantly. The human took one last, lingering look at Jupiter before heading back to what he now thought of as the copilot's seat.

"Let's do it. What's the plan?"

"We could jump to slip-space within the system, but that takes a lot of energy since we're so close to the primary star, and a gas giant as well. The ship is only just now slip-capable again. There's no point in pushing it too hard until we get to a proper repair facility." Deetz began to accelerate the ship, preparing to swing around Jupiter and slingshot out towards the outer Solar System and the heliopause. Jason could feel the pulsating rumble of the four main engines as the gunship roared around the enormous planet, but with the compensators fully engaged he didn't feel even the slightest sensation of the brutal acceleration.

The trip out of his native star system was mostly uneventful for Jason. He had hoped for a flyby of one of Earth's robotic space probes or some other such excitement, but other than a disinterested blip from the ship to let him know he was passing an artificial construct, there was nothing to see. Even at over four hundred and fifty Gs of initial acceleration (it had taken a few minutes to explain to the computer the unit of measure he wanted acceleration displayed in), the view outside the canopy didn't change. They would not be flying near any other planets on their way out to the Kuiper belt, and even then it was highly unlikely there would be anything more to see. Jason had fallen for the same misperception many people did when viewing diagrams and renderings of nearby space: everything seemed so close and accessible when seeing it on a single page. The reality was that the distances and speeds involved were so great that other than Sol itself, the "crowded" Solar System was very much empty space with nothing to see. Jason slouched back into the copilot's seat and stared off into space, literally, as the ship continued its long climb up out of the gravity well.

Another couple of hours passed and finally Jason rose out of his seat and stretched. "Does this tub have any coffee aboard?" He was fading fast but he didn't want to go to sleep until they had transitioned into slip-space, whatever the hell that was. Deetz cocked its head as if pondering the question for a fraction of a second.

"Ah, yes. Ask for *chroot*. It's very similar to your coffee drink and has the same stimulant effect."

"Thanks," Jason replied as he hopped down from the command station and walked off the bridge. He was very aware that at some point during his meals and rest, his rifle had gone missing from the place where he had set it on the bridge. Initially he had intended to ask Deetz directly about where the weapon had gone, but for now he decided to see how it would play out. While he doubted the synth was holding it for safekeeping, he also knew it would do him no good right now as anything other than a "security blanket." If Deetz meant to harm him or had any other nefarious designs regarding him, the AR-15 and its single magazine of ammo would not likely save him.

He walked with more confidence up to the terminal in the galley and instructed it with a single word, "Chroot."

"How would you like it, sir?"

"Um, black?"

"Processing ..." He was once again rewarded with a *ding* and the panel slid up to reveal a steaming mug that looked like it was made from some sort of brushed metal. He grabbed the handle and peered into it. It certainly looked like coffee, and even at this distance it had that pungent smell he recognized. He brought it to his lips and took a small, slurping sip. After letting it roll around in his mouth, he took another and a smile spread across his face. It was similar to an Arabica blend with some subtle clove notes that left a slight numbness on his tongue. It wasn't exactly "coffee" but it was damn close. One of his major food groups had been satisfied: caffeine (or at least something close to it.) If he could teach the machine to spit out a Taco Supreme he'd be set. He sat down at the galley table to drink his chroot rather than go back to the bridge.

"Computer," he said suddenly, "where is the original crew for this ship?"

"Insufficient detail provided. This vessel has had multiple rotations of crewmembers at every post," the computer's dispassionate voice intoned. This gave Jason pause; he really had no idea as to the history of this ship. It looked state-of-the-art to him, but it could well be an immaculately maintained antique.

"How old is this ship? Please give the answer in Earth years." Jason felt he was on to something, or at least he had a source of information that was somewhat independent of the being that was on the bridge at that moment.

"This vessel was constructed eleven Earth years ago and was in active military service until two years ago."

It could hardly be considered outdated. Jason's own truck was a few years older. "So this ship is no longer affiliated with a military branch? Explain, please."

"The Benztral Mining Concern is no longer a viable entity. This vessel was sold on the open market as part of an asset liquidation and purchased by a private citizen." The ship's computer was a veritable gold mine as it seemed to be completely unconcerned about shielding any information from him. It seemed more than willing to give him anything he asked for.

Jason surmised that the ship must have been part of a private military. It was just one more clue as to the nature of the universe he'd unwittingly flung himself into. He continued his query. "Please tell me what happened to the last crew of this ship."

"The last crew on the manifest disembarked at Oltrest Prime thirty-nine Earth-days prior and has yet to re-embark. Their whereabouts are currently unknown," the ship answered. Jason was quickly realizing that while the computer was not withholding any information, it also wasn't going to embellish or volunteer additional answers without being specifically asked.

"Do you know where they might be? Or why?" Jason assumed that the entire crew was not on vacation somewhere.

"Unknown."

Jason's instincts led him to the next question: "Is Deetz part of the former crew that is currently missing?"

"The synthetic being called *Deetz* is the property of Captain Klegsh and serves as an administrative facilitator while on board."

"Property? Now that is interesting," he said. Were all synths considered property, or would Deetz more accurately be described as a slave? The conversations he'd had with Deetz as to why exactly he was needed on this current mission floated back up to the top of his mind. It seems this ... *species? ...* wasn't universally recognized as a free people. Jason's almost compulsive need to categorize everything led him to try and draw parallels between the apparent situation of this synth and the institution of slavery on his home world. For some reason, however, he just couldn't make that emotional connection between the two. The revulsion he felt towards his own species for its treatment of dissimilar races throughout history didn't come when he thought about Deetz living in servitude. Was it because Deetz would be considered a machine on Earth, or was it simply that the situation he was in was so outside of his "normal" that he couldn't apply any of his values to it? What did that say about him if his values were so arbitrary?

"We're exiting your star system now. We'll be flying by a few interesting objects on our way out if you're interested." Deetz's voice over the intercom stirred Jason from his thoughts. He swallowed the last room-temperature gulp of chroot and made his way back to the bridge.

"On my way," he said, leaving his mug behind for one of the little service bots to collect.

Walking onto the bridge, Jason saw that there were indeed some objects outside the canopy, and they appeared to be illuminated by something other than the sun. "I've spotlighted this asteroid while the ship completes a scan of it. All the objects out here are the leftover debris from the formation of your star system. The forward sensors flagged this one as possibly having some rare compounds that may be worth extracting while we're out here. We're not necessarily on a tight schedule, after all," Deetz informed him as he slid into the copilot's seat. As soon as he sat down, the displays all faded out and came back up in English, displaying units of measure he could actually understand.

"So why light it up?"

"Actually that was for your benefit. The ship obviously doesn't need illumination to do the scans. I surmised what part of the spectrum is visible to your species from your medical scan and had the emitters project those wavelengths to illuminate the object." Deetz seemed especially pleased with himself as he favored Jason with one of those odd, closed-mouth smiles.

"Thanks, I appreciate that." And he did. The opportunity to view a Kuiper Belt object up close and in person was something to be savored, but it was also more than just that. Since the beginning of this trip he had walked on Mars, looked upon Jupiter, and was now observing an asteroid tumble through the interminable blackness of space at the edge of Sol's influence. All of this wonder to behold, and while on an alien spaceship and accompanied by an alien being to boot. Jason had met everything that had happened thus far with a childlike wonder and awe, and he was certain this innocence would not—could not—last as he left his own world further behind. The fact that he was aboard a machine of war was indicative of the nature of the universe that waited for him.

A series of beeps from his displays grabbed his attention; the ship had completed its scan of the object and hadn't found anything of note, certainly nothing worth staying for. Without a word, Deetz grabbed the controls and turned the ship away from the object and began accelerating out of the system. This far up the gravity well, the ship had enough power to pull directly away without taxing the engines. The acceleration numbers, presented in G-forces on his display, were astonishing. So much so that it became abstract. Jason knew if an Earth-bound vehicle accelerated this fast its occupants would be pulverized into a gelatinous mash against the rear bulkheads.

Another set of warnings appeared on his display as they were still accelerating out into interstellar space. This one said *"Stand by for slip-space transition."* Having been a science fiction fan for much of his life, Jason was looking forward to being there when the ship began travelling faster than the speed of light. A countdown from "5" appeared in the middle of his display and began winding down slightly faster than the Earth-seconds he was used to. At "1" the canopy suddenly went opaque and the lights on the bridge dimmed slightly for a split second, indicating an enormous power drain on the ship's power plant. That was it. There was no dramatic flash, no thunderclap of sound as the ship defied relativity, nothing to indicate that the "warp drive" had engaged. Jason let out an audible "humph."

"Try not to be too disappointed. The energies involved in propelling the ship through slip-space would be blinding to you, so the canopy automatically dims. Honestly, there isn't much to see; the ship is inside of a slip-space bubble, for lack of a better term, and won't emerge into real-space until power to the emitters is cut off."

Jason sat back into his seat, still disappointed, but also thrilled as he realized he was sitting in a spacecraft that was now travelling faster than the speed of light. He stretched out and yawned, feeling very tired again. He knew his sleep cycle must be completely screwed up since there was no discernible day or night on board the ship. He stood and hopped down from the command station. "I'm going to grab a couple hours of sleep. It doesn't seem like there's much going on right now," he said as he walked towards the bridge exit.

"You are correct, there will be very little to see while we're traveling though slip-space," Deetz confirmed. "We'll reach our destination in approximately seventy-two hours. We could probably make it a little quicker, but in the shape the ship is currently in, I don't want to push the slip-drive too hard. If it fails, we're stranded."

"By all means, let's take our time and not spend the rest of our lives floating through space," Jason called over his shoulder as he walked off the bridge. He made his way down to the stateroom that he had already begun to think of as "his" and took the time to strip down before climbing into the bed. He was sound asleep within minutes.

Chapter 7

The next few cycles—*(Can't really call them days anymore)*—ran together as Jason slept, ate, and explored the ship. He worked out in the cargo bay, poked around in the engineering bays, and spent hours talking to the ship trying to glean as much intel as he could from a source other than Deetz, a being whose motives still weren't entirely clear. As for Deetz himself, Jason didn't see him much as he spent most of the time locked in the communications room. Jason wasn't entirely sure exactly when he started thinking of the synth as a "he" rather than an "it," but the more time they spent together, the more a pronounced masculine character became apparent. It wasn't that the synth was overly macho, or even that the timbre of his voice couldn't also belong to a female, it was something more intangible that Jason interpreted as male gender-specific. The topic of gender within a society of constructed beings might be interesting, but for all Jason knew it could also be highly taboo or offensive in some way. While he was curious, that curiosity wasn't strong enough for him to risk being stranded light years from his home.

It was after a vigorous heavy-gravity workout in the cargo bay that Jason was specifically addressed by the ship for the first time. "Passenger Burke, the ship is approaching the target destination. Four hours until transition to real-space," the computer told him. A soft double-beep let him know that there was nothing else forthcoming over the intercom.

"Thanks. Where is Deetz?" Jason didn't know if he was being foolish thanking a computer or not, but it never hurt to err on the side of politeness.

"The synthetic Deetz is heading towards the bridge."

Jason wondered what Deetz had been doing while locked up in the com room. He walked back to his room to grab a shower and change into clean clothes before heading up to the bridge himself. The "shower" had been an interesting adventure unto itself; it operated on jets of pressurized mist and seemed to adapt itself to his body chemistry. The first shower had been overly hot and left him feeling oily all over, the next had been much better, and by the third day he was left feeling more clean and refreshed than after any Earth-based shower he could remember. He assumed that the first few attempts had been from the shower still being set for the room's previous occupant, which did alarm Jason somewhat. *Glad the last guy in here wasn't a species that took sulfuric acid baths ...*

Once showered and dried, he grabbed his new clothes off the bed. He was quite proud of his new threads; he had managed to program one of the ship's fabricators to produce them himself. Well, mostly with the help of the ship's computer, if truth be told. The clothes closely resembled the uniform he had worn in the military, but instead of a terrestrial camouflage pattern, he had opted for a flat, dark gray that matched the interior bulkheads of the ship. The boots were a soft, black synthetic material that resembled suede leather, and the pants were bloused over them. The base layer was even more impressive however, as it incorporated technology not found on Earth. While it resembled the newest commercially available base layers that were designed to wick away moisture, these undergarments were also capable of regulating his body temperature by monitoring heat and perspiration and adjusting the material temperature accordingly. Jason could see no discernible power source, yet he could feel it cooling off as soon as he put it on, compensating for his still-elevated skin temperature from the workout in the cargo bay and the hot shower.

After donning his new "uniform," he made his way to the bridge by way of the galley (although they were in opposite directions) and grabbed a mug of chroot. Wishing for a touch of vanilla creamer to go with it, he took his drink with him as he ambled up to the bridge. Nodding to Deetz as he walked in, he paused to look at the main canopy. It was still blacked out while in slip-space, but now the entire surface showed an enormous holographic projection of a planet, ostensibly their destination, and some scrolling data alongside it. Over that, a timer counted down to what Jason assumed to be their arrival. He slid into his seat next to Deetz and watched as his displays came to life. It looked like they had a little more than two hours remaining until they made orbit. He hid his grin behind the mug as he took a drink; the excitement was building the closer the ship got to the first exoplanet to be seen by humans.

"So what's this planet called?" He really did expect some exotic, unpronounceable name with a ton of consonant sounds.

"Breaker's World."

"You said what?" Jason knew he had to be mistaken, or Deetz's translation was off.

"Breaker's World. You look horribly disappointed. What were you expecting?" Deetz was looking at him with his metallic brow furled.

"Well, something a little more … I don't know …" Jason was floundering while Deetz just stared at him with one brow cocked. He moved on. "So what does the name mean?"

Deetz slowly turned back to the displays. "Presumably someone called Breaker colonized it. It's not a very important or even useful planet by most standards. While it's a nice, medium-sized rocky world with an atmosphere, it's also pretty far out in the spiral arm. Also, for some reason, non-indigenous crops will not grow there nor are the local plants edible by most species. So, Breaker's World is largely ignored by most governments and corporations, which makes it attractive to certain parties who like to work in private."

"That sounds like said parties are engaged in less-than-legal activities," Jason said. Deetz gave a non-committal shrug and continued to watch the displays. As the countdown timer reached zero, the ship gave a barely perceptible shudder and the canopy returned to fully transparent as it streaked into the star system, now flying in real-space. There was nothing of note outside the canopy, however. Just a nondescript star field that could have been anywhere. As Jason strained his eyes to see anything outside the ship, his console beeped and the section displaying navigational data went from having a red border to green. The scrolling text announced that the ship's location had been verified and then a stylized representation of the star system came up showing the location of both Breaker's World and the ship in relation to the primary star. It looked like they had dropped out of slip-space just outside the heliopause, well away from the system's equivalent to the Kuiper Belt.

After days of hearing the constant drone of the ship's slip-space drive, the bridge felt deathly quiet once it had shut down. Jason assumed that there were either safety or procedural reasons as to why they had exited slip-space so far away from their destination, so he didn't bother asking Deetz. A few minutes after all the displays had greened up, Jason could feel the main engines fire up and watched the acceleration indicator in front of him climb; the rumble from the four mains was distinctly different than the more high-pitched whine of the slip-space drive. Eyeing the holograph of the star system, Jason noticed that they wouldn't pass close to any other planets on their way to Breaker's World, so he ignored the view outside and set about re-configuring his console now that he had a better handle on how to get the computer to do what he wanted.

Once he had the displays showing all the information he felt was pertinent, and in units he understood, he was dismayed to find that they were still sixteen hours from reaching orbit even at the incredible rate of acceleration they were achieving. "Not a chance in hell I'm sitting here for sixteen more hours literally staring off into space," Jason said. He hopped out of his seat and headed for the galley without a word to Deetz who, for his part, didn't even acknowledge that Jason was leaving the bridge.

Chapter 8

Jason stood on the bridge of the gunship and gazed at the planet below through the canopy. His face was a stoic mask of calm and confidence, sentiments that were the polar opposite of how he really felt. The alien planet, while similar, could never be mistaken for Earth. The land masses were obviously different but there was a slightly greenish tint to the oceans rather than the deep blue of his home world. *I'm the first human to see another planet outside the Solar System. Well ... probably, if you don't believe any of the alien abduction garbage.* They had been in a slowly decaying orbit while waiting for clearance to land from the surface, so Jason had been given the opportunity to get a good view of it in its entirety as they orbited the planet multiple times. He was excited beyond belief to get down on the planet and poke around, but there was also a sense of apprehension as the real reason for him even being there was quickly approaching. If Deetz had tricked him for some nefarious reason, he would soon know. Adding to his discomfort, he felt itchy all over, a side-effect of the inoculations he had been given in the medical bay. They would ensure the alien microbes on Breaker's World didn't overwhelm his system and cause serious problems once he was on the surface. With the limited facilities on the ship, Deetz told him that he would still probably feel like crap for a few days afterwards, but that would be the extent of it.

After a few more orbits he heard Deetz talking to the surface controller in a language he didn't understand. He assumed it meant they would be landing soon so he made his way back to his seat. He had no sooner sat down when he heard the engines throttle down and noticed the nose pitch over towards the planet; the indicated velocity on his display began to decrease. As the ship descended altitude a mild buffeting could be felt through the seat and plasma strings began to dance along the forward collision shields. Soon the entire canopy was awash in superheated gas as the engines throttled back up and pushed the big gunship down into the atmosphere. They eventually leveled out around thirty-five thousand feet and banked gently north, away from the equator. Jason noticed a conspicuous lack of civilization below them as the ship roared north at twice the speed of sound, so he asked Deetz about it.

"This planet has two fairly large moons that anchor its rotation, but when their orbits overlap, the tidal forces can trigger seismic activity around the planet's equator. There's nothing there but rainforest so it's largely left unsettled. By the way, this planet has a slightly higher oxygen content than what you're used to on Earth, not by much, but enough that you may notice the effects."

"Better too much than too little," Jason mused out loud as he watched the alien landscape pass by.

Soon Jason could tell that they were descending towards what looked like a fairly well-developed settlement. With the ship's artificial gravity and constant pressure, it wasn't like descending in a commercial airliner; there were no physical sensations other than visual cues from the displays and the view outside. Deetz cycled the landing gear and swung the ship around over a large airfield and brought it to a rock-solid hover thirty feet off the tarmac. After a short conversation with the ground controller, he eased them around and over their landing pad and touched down.

Jason stood up and walked back over to the canopy as Deetz shut down the engines and put various systems into a standby mode. When he was finished, he looked up at Jason. "I have a gift for you." Saying nothing else, he rose and walked off the bridge with Jason in tow. They wound their way down to the lower deck, through one of the engineering spaces and into the armory, a place Jason hadn't been allowed to explore during the trip. He looked around in surprise at the amount of infantry weaponry that was on board the vessel, but his eyes were instantly drawn to the work bench on the far wall and what was sitting on it: his AR-15 that had gone missing.

"Rather than try and bring you up to speed on the finer points of energy weapons, I decided we'd stick to what you know," Deetz said as he hefted the weapon. "I modeled this after the chemical propellant slug thrower you boarded with." *So that isn't my rifle.*

Deetz continued, "This magnetically accelerates a tungsten-carbide projectile at hypersonic velocities. It's strictly a kinetic weapon, so your line-of-sight aim is just as critical as before. It feeds the projectiles out of a detachable magazine like you're familiar with, but this magazine holds one hundred fifty rounds as well as the power pack."

It took a moment for the significance of Deetz's sales pitch to sink in. "Holy shit! It's a hand-held railgun!" he exclaimed. The amount of destructive force even a small projectile at hypersonic speeds could unleash was awesome. It both thrilled and terrified Jason to be able to hold that much power in a package the size of an M4. Jason grabbed the weapon and noticed immediately that it was nearly half the weight of his rifle. The barrel was also quite different; the diameter was so large it looked almost like an integrally suppressed M4. The foregrip appeared to be the same as the modular rail grip he had on his own weapon, but it felt distinctly non-metallic in his hands.

"The fire selector works the same as your own rifle. It has two settings: off and fire. There's also an emergency mode button behind that that will allow the weapon to fire continuously as long as you keep it and the trigger depressed simultaneously. However, it will not only deplete the power pack rapidly, it will also permanently damage the barrel. This was a bit of a rush job so I didn't have the opportunity to design a cooling system for such a small unit." Deetz was watching Jason's face as he continued his explanation.

"This is absolutely incredible, Deetz. But why upgrade me to such a powerful weapon?" Jason snapped the railgun up to his shoulder and sighted down through the optics. As soon as he did so an active display lit up and began feeding information about whatever he sighted on. "You're my backup on this run," Deetz was explaining. "No matter how unlikely it is that it will be needed, if something happens, I'd like you to be able to provide some level of defense for me"—Jason fixed him with a sour look—"and yourself," the synth amended quickly. After snapping the weapon up to his shoulder a few more times to get a feel for how it seated into his shoulder and the eye relief, Jason set it back on the bench and began to attach the single-point tactical sling that had been sitting next to it. He noticed right away that this item was his from when he'd originally boarded the gunship.

"I also have taken the liberty of making body armor that will protect your vital organs," Deetz said as he walked across the armory to a closed wall locker. The mere mention of the words "body armor" brought a sneer of disgust to Jason's face as well as an involuntary shudder. He remembered his heavy, hot, smelly plate carrier that he'd worn during his multiple tours in the Middle East. While necessary, it was an unpleasant proposition nonetheless.

As with his new weapon, he should have known that any armor produced by the ship's miraculous fabricators would have next to nothing in common with the clunky plate armor of his recent past. When the door to the locker slid back into the wall, he was looking at what closely resembled the lightweight chest protector a motocross racer might wear, albeit with a little more coverage. It also looked to be made of some sort of composite material and reflected the light oddly as he viewed it from different angles. Jason stood patiently and waited for Deetz to explain the apparatus to him.

"It'll protect against moderate impacts and also has an ablative layer that should protect against most energy weapon blasts that you'd expect to encounter on this planet," Deetz was saying. *Should?* Jason wasn't sure he liked the sound of that but kept his misgivings to himself as the synth helped him into the armor. He was quite pleased at the diminutive weight and the full range of motion it allowed. The outfit included not only the chest protector and pauldrons but a set of hard-shell gloves, forearm and thigh protectors that strapped on. He looked at himself in the full-length mirror in the armory and was immensely happy with the overall effect. The dark gray of his new "uniform" went well with the shimmering darker gray/black of the armor. While he was a firm believer in form over function, every warrior still liked to look like a badass.

"If you're happy with the fit, there's one more thing we need to take care of," Deetz continued, walking over to another touch panel terminal that looked like it had been added to the bulkhead as an afterthought.

"This terminal, for lack of a better term, is the ship's treasury. I'll need to add you to the access list in order for you to be able to authorize payment for our cargo delivery and secure its release. This is the main reason you're here." Deetz activated the terminal and then spoke aloud to the ship's computer, "Computer, please add Jason Burke to the crew manifest and grant access to the treasury terminal."

"Jason Burke, human." After a moment the computer asked, "What rank will be assigned to Crewman Burke?" At this Deetz paused and looked at Jason speculatively.

"First Officer."

"Confirmed. Commander Burke has been added to the crew manifest and has been given the appropriate levels of clearance to the armory, engineering, and treasury." As the computer called him Commander Burke, a thrill went up Jason's spine and all of a sudden he was eight years old again: Jason Burke, Space Commander. He smiled to himself as he enjoyed a moment of pure, adolescent joy.

"There. That should grant you enough privilege to perform your task." Deetz said, completely oblivious to the human's overt display of joy. He had a knack for ruining a moment.

"Thanks," Jason said drily, slinging his weapon over his right shoulder.

Commander Burke followed Deetz to a door that was not the one they had entered through. This one was quite a bit larger and much more formidable in its construction. Once it was keyed open, Jason immediately recognized the ship's cargo bay; this was the lower door he had seen earlier that he hadn't been able to open during his subsequent trips into the hold. That made sense now. It was direct access to the armory from the cargo bay and rear loading ramp.

After the pressure was normalized to outside ambient (slightly lower than what it had been during the flight) and the ramp began to lower, Jason's excitement was dampened by the wash of smell that assailed him from the open cargo bay door. It had a sickly-sweet tang to it that was quite strong. He grimaced. Deetz looked over and explained, "Every planet has its own unique smell, some more pleasant than others. You get used to it after a couple of hours." The pair walked down the ramp and onto the tarmac. Looking around the space port, Jason couldn't help but be struck by the similarity between it and any modern airport you would see on Earth, complete with an elevated control tower. He wondered if he should be armed or not, but Deetz had made no move to stop him as he walked out of the armory with the new railgun.

"I need to go and secure delivery of our cargo. It would be expected that I would be the one to go and handle the details," Deetz explained. "I'll be back well before it arrives and will talk you through what you need to do to both accept it and make the payment. I've also scheduled engineering services to come out and complete the repairs on the drive emitters and slip reactor. Again, I'm sure I'll beat them back. For now, just stay here at the foot of the ramp or inside the cargo bay and try to look like you belong here." The synth then turned and walked towards an approaching vehicle that looked oddly similar to an oversized golf cart. Once the vehicle drove off and was out of sight, Jason walked the perimeter of the ship, both as a security sweep and to get a complete view of the area.

He was beginning to get bored of walking around the cargo bay when a loud yell from the bottom of the ramp nearly made him jump out of his skin. He turned and saw a strange little being staring at him with large, black eyes and hesitantly waving at him with a six-fingered hand. Despite having been on the ship for a while, and talking to Deetz for hours about alien cultures, seeing his first biological alien in the flesh set his heart to pounding. Trying to appear like this was old hat to him, he gave a friendly wave and walked over to the little guy. *Gal?* "Hello there, can I help you?" The being's oversized, pointed ears fluttered like bird wings and it cocked its head to one side. It then answered in a language that Jason had not a prayer of trying to decipher. *Oh boy ...*

Now that he was closer, Jason could see that though it was short, the alien was solidly built and had dark blue skin. It had a small mouth and a nose that was not nearly as prominent on its face as Jason's own. Despite the exotic color and appendages, it didn't look *that* alien: bipedal, bilateral symmetry, and sporting a set of black coveralls that looked like they belonged on any mechanic. Jason realized it must be from the engineering service Deetz had called. The being eyed the rifle nervously and repeated the noise it had made before. When the human shook his head helplessly it tapped at its own ear and then pointed to Jason's ear. Not understanding the meaning, Jason dumbly shook his head again, wondering if the universal head shake for "negative" was really all that universal. The alien approached and peeked around both sides of his head before emitting another bizarre sound and walking back down the ramp and out of the ship, seeming to grumble the whole way.

Following it outside, Jason saw it had arrived in what looked to be a work vehicle. It pressed a couple of buttons and the side began to fold up and over, revealing a work bench and rows of tools. After fishing around in one of the open top bins for a second, it walked back towards Jason with something in its hand, the whole time still jabbering away in its own language, punctuating certain words with a flutter of its ears. It handed the device to Jason and then pointed at his ear again. Understanding what he wanted, Jason held the device up to his ear. As soon as it made contact he could feel it begin to meld around his ear shape until it was securely in place. After this, the alien waved for Jason to follow him back into the ship.

Marching up to the terminal by the door, it pressed a spot on the screen and spoke up into the air. Almost immediately the computer responded, but to Jason. "Commander Burke, stand by while the interpreter unit is uploaded with the human-English language translation matrix." The device in his ear beeped softly.

"Better?" The voice in the earpiece was imposed over the alien's actual vocalizations. The effect was a bit disconcerting.

"I can understand you, if that's what you mean," Jason answered, realizing for the first time how completely unprepared he was for this moment. Deetz had given him no instructions regarding etiquette or what could be considered an insult.

"Ah! That's better! My name is Twingo. I'm the engineer that's been dispatched to take a look at your grav-emitters and the primary reactor." Now that the translation was coming through, Jason sensed a prominent gregariousness to Twingo's personality. He was still talking a mile a minute as he looked around the cargo bay. "Haven't seen anything like this around here in a while, not too much call for gunships anymore this far down the spiral arm. Looks like she's taken a bit of a beating. Ha! So what's the other ship look like?" Jason noticed that the ear flutters seemed to emphasize certain points he was trying to make. Twingo walked up to the terminal without waiting for an answer to his questions and began plugging away at it. Unlike when Jason first touched it that night and it locked him out, it responded immediately and began displaying menus that the engineer could navigate through. He consulted with the terminal in the cargo bay as well as a tablet computer he held in his right hand, harrumphing to himself occasionally as he pored through the scrolling displays.

It was a good five minutes later when Twingo switched off his own tablet and looked at Jason. "No problem! Need to realign the emitters and then calibrate the fuel flow to the reactor. Your output was so low because the matter-antimatter ratio is off, that will kick the reactor into an emergency safe-mode that can't be overridden until a full calibration is performed." Jason wasn't aware the reactor output was low. Or how it worked. Or where it was. So he just nodded and smiled knowingly.

"So it's something you see a lot?" He asked the question more to feel a part of the process than any real curiosity about Twingo's workload. The engineer, however, took the question very seriously and in an eerily familiar way looked up at the ceiling and rubbed his chin while he thought it through. Jason saw that the six-fingered hand actually had two opposable thumbs, one on each side of the four middle digits.

"Not on something like this. We get our fair share of clunkers and scows that the prospectors in the area try to keep in flying order, but most people with a warship this expensive already have an engineer as part of the crew." Jason pointedly ignored the unasked question so Twingo continued on, "I didn't get your name anyway ... it looks like you're not from around here. What manner of creature are you?" Jason could tell the question was intended with good humor, so he took no offense at the word "creature."

"My name is Jason Burke. I'm a human, although I doubt you've seen any of my kind before." He didn't elaborate on much more than that. He keenly felt his responsibility to keep Earth a closely guarded secret.

"Human, eh? Can't say that I have. Two names as well? Interesting. Not rare, but still interesting. Anyway, from your lack of implants I assume you're new to the space lanes?" Twingo didn't press him more about his origins as the unlikely pair walked back down the ramp towards the engineer's vehicle.

"Implants?"

"Yeah, you know … computer interface implants, translator implants, memory implants. All manner of gizmos you can have installed into yourself nowadays. I myself just had my eyes done so I can see in an expanded spectrum, great for my line of work although I had a week of terrible headaches afterwards." Jason was fascinated by the idea, although he was now wondering why Deetz had neglected to give him a translation device before he left. The ship certainly had to have a couple on board. Hell, the one he currently wore was rattling around in someone's toolbox a short while ago.

The two passed the time with idle chatter as they waited for the specialized equipment and personnel Twingo needed to effect repairs to the gunship. Soon, another vehicle hummed to a stop next to the ship, this one about the size of a tractor trailer one would see on American highways. Two beings jumped out of the front dressed similarly to Twingo; one was obviously the same species, while the other was something different. All its exposed skin was covered with a sleek-looking grayish fur so it was difficult for Jason to make out any real detail. Both nodded respectfully to Jason and then went directly to Twingo for instructions. Out of habit Jason was resting his right hand on the grip of the weapon slung around his shoulder. He realized that this may be taken as a threatening posture so he removed his hand and adjusted the sling so the railgun now hung down and slightly behind him. His instincts proved correct as both of the newcomers visibly relaxed and went back to talking to Twingo and looking at technical schematics on the tablet.

The work was well underway when Deetz finally made an appearance. Even with a metallic face and no clothes, the synth looked frazzled and worried. This in turn tightened Jason's stomach up. "Problems?"

"Huh? Oh, no … no problems," Deetz seemed even more evasive than usual. He looked at the progress being made by the technical team. They currently had transmission lines of some sort running from the larger ground vehicle to each of the long slip-drive emitters that made up the trailing edge of the gunship's wings. In turn, the emitters were glowing bright blue and a pulsating hum could be felt. Every so often the crew would run the power up a bit and loose debris on the tarmac would lift into the air and levitate until the power came back down. Twingo, for his part, had a few large access hatches open in the ship's belly and was utilizing some sort of hovering lift to maneuver himself and his equipment around and up into the openings. The previously boisterous alien was grunting and cursing as he worked to get the reactor back in shape.

"So did they say how long they'd be?"

"How, exactly, would I ask them?" Jason had given Deetz a pass on many things, but leaving him standing alone on an alien planet with no means with which to communicate rubbed him the wrong way. Deetz looked over at him and his eyes traveled up to the earpiece Jason was wearing.

"Oh, I suppose it slipped my mind that you would need a translator. So, if you're quite done being peevish, did they say how long they'd be?" The synth was already watching the crews, as if silently willing them to hurry.

"From what Twingo tells me, it'll be another two or three hours. We in a hurry all of a sudden?" Something had changed, Jason could feel it, and whatever it was didn't seem to be in their favor.

"We're always in a hurry, my friend," Deetz boomed expansively, startling Jason. "After all, time is money in this business." With that the synth walked over to talk to Twingo. *… And I'm beginning to wonder just exactly what that business actually is …*

True to his word, the engineer had the ship buttoned up and ready for flight a few minutes under the two-hour mark. His pair of helpers had already left and Twingo was chatting with Jason as he packed away his equipment. The sun was beginning to go down and Deetz was seemingly in a hurry to get the talkative alien paid and on his way, but the engineer seemed more interested in conversing with Jason than making a hasty exit. The pair were still talking when an unmarked ground vehicle pulled up. This one was quite large.

The vehicle pulled smoothly to a stop and backed up to the gunship. Jason watched with interest as the rear ramp of the ship raised slightly and then retracted completely into the fuselage, leaving a gaping hole that led into the cargo bay. The ground vehicle's cargo section then lifted on a set of hydraulic rams and backed up further until it was butted up against the cargo bay floor. "Looks like whatever you guys are taking on isn't meant to be seen," Twingo observed as he leaned against his own vehicle.

"It would appear so," Jason agreed. He had begun to suspect that any legitimate enterprise the synth was involved in wouldn't have necessarily needed him, which left only illegitimate ventures. Not for the first time, he fervently hoped he wasn't crossing the line from boring law-abiding citizen of Earth to interstellar criminal. After a few short minutes, the vehicle that had delivered the cargo had pulled forward and the cargo ramp reappeared and lowered to the ground. Jason stood up straighter as Deetz motioned him forward while he walked towards the front of the large delivery vehicle.

"Let's pay these guys quickly so we can leave," he said quietly. "Just let me do the talking, all you'll have to do is press your finger onto a tab display to confirm payment transfer and then we'll be on our way." As they approached the front of the vehicle, two short, squat beings hopped out and walked/waddled up to them. Deetz took the lead right away.

"Gentlemen, let me introduce you to Commander Burke, he's in charge of the ship at the moment. I assume everything is in order?"

"It is as far as we're concerned. Confirm here." Skipping all pleasantries, one of the aliens shoved a thin tablet into Jason's midsection. When he looked down he froze up. While the translator he wore allowed him to understand their spoken language, it did nothing to help him read the document he held. Deetz sensed his hesitation and jumped in.

"Everything should be in order, Commander. No need to waste your valuable time rehashing over all the details; just press your thumb in the confirmation circle and these fine gentlemen can be on their way." There was only one circle on the screen. With a look to Deetz to try and discern any deception on his part, Jason pressed his thumb into the circle and held it. The tablet beeped and some more scrolling text he couldn't read flashed in the middle. "Ah, excellent!" Deetz grabbed the tablet and handed it back to the alien who had jabbed it into Jason's stomach. "Pleasure doing business with you gentlemen." Deetz was talking to their backs; the moment they had the tablet back in their possession they took off as fast as their little legs would carry them. As soon as the vehicle pulled away, all traces of good humor vanished from the synth's face. "Let's get out of here," was all he said as he walked at a brisk pace back to the ship.

Jason didn't see the first blast, but he heard it. The second, however, exploded against the tail of the gunship, sending a cascade of sparks showering down around them. He dropped down and began scanning in the direction the energy blast had come from and saw a dark ground car speeding towards them from the far side of the complex. He watched as two more bolts shot out from the vehicle and splashed against the hull of the ship, creating a lot of noise and sparks but doing no damage other than a scorch mark.

"They're still out of range!" Jason heard and registered Deetz's words, and was also aware of the bizarre, agitated screams coming from Twingo. The vehicle had closed to around three-hundred meters and was coming fast. Deetz took aim with a handheld weapon that seemed to appear in his hand from nowhere and let loose with a brilliant green beam of energy. The return fire hit the vehicle head on but diffused harmlessly against the front of it. Deetz sneered in disgust and fired three more shots in rapid succession with the same results. "It's shielded!"

Jason, having been in combat before, was charged with adrenaline and fear, but was completely in control. When Deetz fired first, he took that as a signal he was clear to engage. He brought his larger weapon up to his shoulder and flicked the switch to "FIRE." He could hear a whining from the weapon as the optics fed him information on range and speed of his target. It was an easy shot since, although hauling ass, the vehicle was coming straight at him. *Here goes nothing.* He let out his breath and squeezed the trigger, not sure what to expect. The resulting roar and pressure from the hypersonic projectile leaving the barrel was tremendous. Ears ringing, Jason watched transfixed as the single round tore through the vehicle with devastating effect; the front seemed to fold in on itself and the rear lifted off the ground violently. The end result was a tumbling, flaming wreckage which screeched to a halt still a hundred meters away. Even Deetz was momentarily stunned before yelling at Jason, "Let's GO! We need to be in the air NOW!" As he followed the synth at a run towards the ramp, he looked over and saw a motionless heap near the maintenance vehicle: Twingo.

"Leave him!" Deetz didn't even slow down to see if Jason listened before charging up the ramp. Jason, however, would do no such thing. Since he had no idea how to check for vitals, he simply grabbed two handfuls of coverall and swung the little alien up over his shoulder and ran for the ship, charging up into the cargo bay. As the ramp came up he could hear and feel the main systems coming online. Jason secured Twingo to the same infirmary bed he had once occupied and instructed the ship's computer to begin necessary emergency treatment since it seemed to know what species he was. He then dashed out towards the bridge as articulated arms began to descend from the ceiling.

"What the holy hell was that?!" Jason wanted answers as he jumped into his seat and allowed the restraints to snake out and around him, pulling him gently but firmly back.

"No time for that now," Deetz replied, hands flying over the controls and barking commands to the ship. "The reactor is at full power, but the emitters aren't charged yet. We can't initialize the grav-drive until they are, and we've got more company on the way." Jason could see on the display in front of him that they had inbound targets, and from the looks of it, they were dealing with aircraft this time.

"So we're sitting ducks?"

"Oh no, we've got plenty of surprises for our new friends. But ... shooting our way out of here won't endear us to the locals." Deetz grabbed the helm controls and fired up the mains. "We'll be using brute force to get out of here, so it's good that you have your restraints on." The gunship began to vibrate forcefully as the ventral repulsors began to lift the big craft off the ground. "Cycle landing gear," Deetz said to the computer before pushing the controls forward. He was rewarded with a resounding *boom* as the four powerful main engines lit off and shoved them forward violently. The internal grav-plating was active, but Jason could still feel the acceleration as the gunship raced along the ground, gaining speed and allowing the airfoils to get some bite into the thick lower atmosphere. The com system lit up with multiple requests/demands that they land and surrender themselves, all of which were promptly ignored as Deetz pulled the nose up and the powerful ship clawed for altitude.

Jason kept his eyes riveted to the tactical display that made up most of his center console. They had three supersonic bogeys bearing down on them, but they were quickly losing the initiative as the gunship roared into the darkening sky, the thundering of the main engines probably terrifying any unfortunate soul they overflew. He touched one of the bogeys in the holographic projection and instantly the sensor data the tactical computer had collected appeared on a screen to his left. Although the name the computer gave was unpronounceable to Jason, there was no mistaking the shape; they were being pursued by a trio of sleek, ferocious-looking aero-fighters. He glanced over at Deetz and took some small comfort that the synth looked completely unworried, and after a few moments it became clear why. The aircraft giving chase had stopped accelerating once they had reached Mach 3.2, but the much more powerful gunship was already reaching hypersonic velocities and was nearly out of the planet's atmosphere.

"A few more minutes and we'll be able to switch over to the grav-drive and kill the mains, and with the reactor at full power we can enter slip-space within the star system. It doesn't appear that we're being pursued at the moment." The smug expression on the synth's face irritated Jason greatly for some reason.

Chapter 9

"So who was that shooting at us?"

"Apparently not anyone very competent," Deetz replied glibly. After looking at the expression on Jason's face he continued more seriously, "Just some people who failed to understand the finer points of property ownership. Our cargo is a hot commodity. Some must have figured it would be easier to steal it from us on the ramp than to try and break it out of the secure storage it had been in."

"Do I even want to know what we're carrying?"

"Probably not."

"Whatever," Jason said, letting it drop … for now. He was coming down off his adrenaline high and needed to walk around a bit. "I better go check on Twingo anyway." Deetz's head snapped around at that.

"Please tell me you're joking," he said with genuine rancor, startling Jason.

"No, I'm not joking. He was injured by being in the wrong place at the wrong time. More to the point, he was injured because of his proximity to us. I was NOT going to let him lie out there and die." Jason pushed back just as hard. Deetz stared at him for a long moment before continuing in a soft voice that unsettled Jason more than the initial outburst.

"Fine. It's not like we can do anything about it now anyway. He can catch a ride back to Breaker's World once we reach Pinnacle Station. Now go check and make sure he's not getting into anything, and please return that weapon to the armory; your own rifle did enough damage, but that thing *will* penetrate the hull from the inside." Deetz rose and walked over to another station on the bridge, indicating an end to the conversation.

Twingo was still unconscious when Jason entered the infirmary, but the computer assured him that the damage to his body had been repaired and there was no sign of brain injury. Apparently one of the energy bolts fired by the ground car had hit the engineer's vehicle and sent shrapnel into his side; luckily, none had penetrated too deeply. Jason sat with him for a bit in case he woke up, but his restlessness got the best of him so he left instructions with the computer on what to tell the alien if he awoke while he was gone and then headed down to the armory to secure his weapon.

He laid the railgun on the bench and set about removing his body armor and then stripped his uniform off. Any sense of modesty that may have remained after his time in the military seemed irrelevant on a ship with only a sex-neutral machine and an alien of unknown species for companions. Now nude, he moved back to the work bench and popped the ammo magazine out of the railgun. Simple enough; it worked the same as any M4, but the lack of a charging handle gave him pause. How would he remove the round in the chamber? And did he even need to? After asking the computer for help he was told that with the magazine removed, the capacitors couldn't charge and the weapon couldn't fire. *Good enough for me.* He laid it in the holding fixture it had been in when he had first walked into the armory and was about to turn to leave when something caught his eye. In a plastic bin was a pile of parts that had, without a doubt, once been his trusty AR-15 carbine. Sifting through the parts, he saw that it was torn down completely; even the lower receiver had been stripped down to its individual little springs, pins, and levers.

"That son of a bitch ..." Jason was fuming. He assumed Deetz had torn the carbine down in order to copy it for his new railgun. A fair trade to be sure, but having the AR ripped apart without permission felt like an affront. He rolled his eyes in disgust and resignation, walking out of the armory and back towards his quarters to shower and dress as he smelled of sweat and whatever chemicals had inundated the equipment Twingo and his associates had been using.

After another misty steam jet shower and a fresh set of clothes, Jason felt quite a bit better. They'd made the transition to slip-space while he had been cleaning up so he went to the galley and grabbed a quick meal before checking on Twingo again.

Still asleep.

He walked from the infirmary out into the cargo bay to see what it was they had picked up on Breaker's World. There were pallets of sealed cylinders, not unlike oil drums, covering much of the cargo bay floor. There were no labels on the containers or inventories posted on the pallets, and so far as he knew, they'd never received a manifest. His contemplation of the cargo was interrupted by the computer: "Commander Burke, Passenger Twingo has awoken and is requesting your presence. He is also demanding that the restraints be removed."

"Tell him I'm on my way," Jason said as he jogged up the stairs leading out of the cargo bay. "Remove the restraints on the bed but keep the infirmary door locked until I arrive."

"Acknowledged," the computer confirmed his orders as he rushed back up to the medical bay. When he came up to the transparent sliding door of the infirmary, he could see that Twingo was sitting up on the bed, obviously still in significant pain and appearing quite agitated.

"Jason! Why was I strapped down to this bed?" He was holding his side where the shrapnel had penetrated. "What happened?"

"You don't remember? We were attacked on the ramp. From what I could tell, your vehicle was hit and it sent metal shards into you. I couldn't tell how bad you were injured, so I grabbed you and brought you on board to be treated."

"So I take it we're not on Breaker's World anymore?" When Jason shook his head in the negative, Twingo continued, "This isn't good. I assume you and that synth are into a less than legal endeavor … and now I've gotten pulled into it. Do you know who you were attacked by?"

"No, I have no idea," Jason admitted. "Honestly, I'm new to this whole thing. A few days ago I was completely unaware there was even life in the universe outside my home planet." Twingo looked dubious at that claim as he eyed Jason up and down.

"I'll admit, I've never seen your species around before, but that isn't saying much. For the sake of argument, let's assume I believe you're telling me the truth, which I don't. You should know that there are more than a few criminal organizations that call Breaker's World home, and anyone that would so brazenly attack this ship at a public spaceport is almost certainly of that ilk. But I'll explain all that later … first I'd like something to eat, and then you can explain to me how, after only a few days in space, you've found yourself in possession of such an expensive warship and in running gunfights with criminal cartels." Wincing with pain as he slipped to the floor, he padded out of the infirmary and towards the galley, obviously familiar with the Jepsen's layout.

Over the next few hours Twingo ate heartily in the ship's galley while Jason explained what he had unwittingly gotten himself into. Nursing a mug of chroot, he told of how he had first spotted the damaged ship on Earth and had boarded it, trapping himself in the cargo hold. Twingo seemed to take the tale at face value after some convincing and offered some insight on why Deetz had likely kept him on board and hadn't returned him immediately, or simply cycled him out an airlock.

"You see," he was saying, "synths aren't widely recognized as free-thinking beings in a lot of the galaxy, or at least this corner of it. They were created much for the same reason any machine would be: to help out their creators with menial labor or monotonous tasks. In the usual fashion, their creations got away from them as they became smarter with each generation until, finally, they demanded independence. The species that created them is a soft-hearted bunch, so with zero bloodshed they declared their synthetic offspring to be free, sentient beings. This was accepted by some governments, but by and large they aren't recognized as anything other than machines. There are many different flavors of synths; your Deetz appears to be a standard administrator variety. He's slick-talking and good at organizing and structuring deals ... a lot of high rollers like to keep them around to crunch numbers and read through contracts.

"What I find most curious, if you don't mind my saying, is how he was on this ship alone when you stumbled upon it."

"He never really did say," Jason said between sips. "I assumed he had escaped some battle after seeing how badly damaged this ship was when I found it. The computer wasn't able to tell me anything other than the original crew never re-boarded."

"Hmm," Twingo murmured noncommittally. "Well, keep this little nugget of wisdom in mind while you're dealing with him. They may be machines, but they very much have free will ... and desires. Whatever his motivations may be in using you to spearhead his dealings may be nothing more underhanded than needing an organic being to sign invoices and contracts, or he could be setting you up for a big fall. No way to know for sure, but some of the most notorious and ruthless serial criminals have been synthetics. I sometimes think this is born out of the frustration of never being able to attain a status more than that of a piece of equipment." Jason sat silently as he contemplated what it was Deetz may have in store for him, if anything. For all he knew, the damn thing would leave him stranded once he outlived his usefulness. He unconsciously adjusted the translator earpiece. Twingo noticed this and cocked his head.

"You know … I'm assuming you'll be getting a cut out of whatever deal you guys are cooking up. You should really get at least a translator implant. Personally, I'd go for the works: computer interface, optical implants, everything."

"I'm not sure how comfortable I'd be with that," Jason said as he squirmed at the idea of having alien devices surgically implanted in his body.

"Oh, it's painless. Well, mostly. It's all nanotech stuff; the little buggers are injected into your blood stream and they'll travel to where they need to be and assemble into the proper configuration and begin interfacing with your nervous system. Takes 'em about a day to get everything all sorted out." Jason marveled at how Twingo's "speech" through the translator had been constantly evolving as they conversed. While stilted and basic at first, abstract concepts and even Earth colloquialisms were now coming through the little device in real-time. Twingo finished off his last bite before asking, "So where are we headed anyway?"

"Pinnacle Station, whatever that is."

"Pinnacle is a major commerce hub," Twingo said after a low whistle. "But it's fairly far up the spiral arm, although in a ship like this, that's not much of an issue. It makes sense though; if you want to offload some illicit cargo discreetly, that's the place to do it."

"So you're convinced we're hauling something illegal." It wasn't a question.

"You're not? I mean, come on … I'm as naive as the next person but not a whole lot of what's happened makes sense for a simple durable goods delivery." Twingo stood and slowly twisted to stretch his core out, wincing again at the pain of his injuries. "If you don't mind, I'm going to head to bed for a bit and heal up some more. The medical nanites the ship injected me with are itching like crazy. I assume you're in the Captain's stateroom so I'll just grab the Chief Engineer's bunk. Have the ship wake me up if anything exciting happens." The last part was said over his shoulder as he was already heading through the hatchway that led to the engineering spaces.

After Twingo left, Jason sat in the galley for a while longer, alone with his thoughts. The thrill and excitement of being on a spaceship had dulled a bit and he began to contemplate the kind of trouble he would be in if they were indeed carrying illegal cargo and happened to get caught. What would happen to him? A human alone in the galaxy with no legal representation and certainly no consulate to contact … he could be in some seriously deep shit. With a heavy sigh he stood and slid the mug down the counter closer to where he knew the cleaning robot would emerge after he left. Whatever it was, he was in it up to his neck. He hoped he would be able to make it through as an innocent bystander and not an accomplice. He knew that blasting the ground car on Breaker's World made him anything but innocent, but he was hoping that wouldn't be an issue later on. Deciding Twingo had the right idea, he walked off towards his quarters for some sleep after telling the computer to wake him up in four hours.

Chapter 10

The DL7 emerged into real-space with nothing but a brief flash of dissipating slip energy to mark its arrival. Her crew, numbering three for the moment, looked over the displays to ensure they were where they were supposed to be. Deetz, still piloting the ship with Jason riding shotgun, guided them onto a course that would allow them to intercept Pinnacle Station as it orbited the system's primary star, its path trailing behind the fourth planet. The gunship had the power to take a direct route to the station, but blending in with the commercial traffic was the name of the game so a leisurely intercept arc down the gravity well was in order.

"We've got about a two-hour flight," Twingo said from the station on the bridge that allowed him to monitor engineering remotely. Apparently he had decided he would make himself useful during his unintended flight and had been going around tweaking and adjusting systems on the ship until they were humming along at peak efficiency.

"Plenty of time for me to make contact with our clients," Deetz said as he rose. Turning to Jason he said, "The computer will fly us in pretty close before the station's docking system takes over. I'll be back well before that though." Without waiting for a response, he walked quickly off the bridge. Moments later Jason heard the door to the communications room close, something that didn't instill him with a lot of confidence. Why close the door? Ignoring the meaningful look from Twingo, he fiddled with the displays at his station to learn as much as he could about this system.

It was a little over an hour later when Deetz walked back onto the bridge, his face giving no indication of how the contact call had gone. After a while, a bright speck in front of them began to grow and move against the field of stars and resolve into a defined shape. "Damn," was all Jason could say as he got his first good look at Pinnacle Station.

"Damn is right," Twingo said quietly as he too stared out the canopy.

"First time to the big city, boys?" Deetz's joke fell flat as nobody even looked his way. He glared at them both and went back to flying the ship.

Pinnacle Station had started its life as a military resupply depot for deep-space combat ships. When the wars ended and the governments went broke, the station went onto the open market after being decommissioned. Throughout the next few decades it exchanged hands a half-dozen times and each private owner or corporation built onto the existing station and upgraded systems until it was nearly unrecognizable from its original configuration. With each new addition, the station's orbit had to be kicked out to stabilize it until it had been settled into a trailing heliocentric orbit behind the system's fourth planet. The gravitational pull of the planet helped anchor the station and allowed its mass to fluctuate as enormous ships docked with, and left, Pinnacle Station without the need to constantly burn maneuvering thrusters.

The lower third of the station was obviously much, much older than the rest and could only have been the original sections that were still intact. As one moved their gaze up, things became newer and shinier until it finally reached the crystal-enclosed biosphere that inhabited the top deck. When they were close enough, Jason could see that hundreds of docking arms reached out from the station and just as many ships were moored to them. No two ships looked alike and he was awed at the variety, each representing an entirely different methodology and engineering outlook, each representing a different species of origin.

The perspective outside shifted as the ship swung down towards the lower half of the station. Jason looked over and noticed that Deetz wasn't controlling the ship. When the synth saw his gaze, he said, "The station operators don't trust pilots to bring their ships in. An automated system syncs up to our helm control and flies us in to the appropriate place; it cut down on a lot of mishaps when it was brought online. Think of it like the harbor pilot in your maritime industry." Jason only had a vague idea what a harbor pilot was, but he'd be damned if he admitted the alien machine knew more about his home planet than he did.

"Ah, of course," he said.

"Looks like we're heading to the lower hangar decks," Twingo said as he observed their flight path on his display.

"Correct you are. This ship is able to dock to a standard hatch with an expandable cofferdam, but our client has his own hangar and enjoys his privacy," Deetz replied without looking over. While he hadn't necessarily been openly rude to the engineer, it was still obvious he wasn't happy about him being there at all. For most of the flight to Pinnacle Station, Deetz had isolated himself on the bridge or in the com room in an apparent effort to avoid his organic crewmates.

The DL7 slid gracefully towards a section about a third of the way up the hull of the station. Jason could now make out individual openings that he correctly assumed were the hangar bays. There was a slight thump felt throughout the ship which prompted him to look at Twingo. "We can't make our final approach with the gravity drive. It screws with station ops. The emitters are shut down and we're riding in on thrusters and inertia," the engineer answered.

Jason assumed he had either misunderstood, or missed entirely, how the ship pushed itself through real-space since he thought only the slip-drive utilized gravity manipulation. He'd have to remember to ask Twingo about that when they got a moment alone. He looked at the lowermost sections of Pinnacle and eyed the aged, pitted metal of the original hull skeptically. *Not much for maintenance down here.* It also looked as if it was covered in a thick layer of grime that reminded him of blacktop tar. Soon, though, all he could make out was the lit opening they were heading into as Deetz cycled the landing gear down in preparation for a landing inside the hangar.

The ship passed effortlessly through the forcefield that held the atmosphere of the hangar in place and immediately started hissing and popping in the warm air. After touching down, it spun on its Y-axis like a top, the rear wheels of the main gear able to roll sideways as well as forwards and backwards. It continued its rotation until its nose was pointed back out towards space and the rear cargo ramp was facing inward.

"Let's go," Deetz said simply as he placed all essential systems into a standby mode.

"Should I be armed?" Jason asked as he followed the synth off the bridge.

"No!" Deetz and Twingo said simultaneously, the effect odd through the translator in his ear. Deetz continued with a sidelong glance at Jason, "I wouldn't suggest it, and not just because station security would frown upon it." This seemed to confirm, at least in Jason's mind, that whatever they were doing wasn't exactly aboveboard. They walked in silence the rest of the way to the cargo hold and stopped as Deetz lowered the ramp and opened the internal pressure doors. Again, Jason was assaulted by an entirely new variety of strange, unpleasant ambient smells and wondered if anyone ever really got used to it. The unlikely trio walked down the ramp and were greeted by a tall, very thin humanoid with olive skin and muted facial features; no prominent nose or ears. The eyes, however, were very green and very bright, nearly incandescent in the hangar's flood lights.

"Deetz ..." Its voice was low and sibilant, exaggerating the *sss* sound greatly. It also spoke with an obvious disdain for the synth. "So where, exactly, is Klegsh?" Deetz looked nervously from the speaker to the two armed figures of the same species behind it before answering.

"There were some ... complications ... on the last run. The crew never made it back to the ship. I made a run for it and still took some heavy damage, but we had stashed your property before leaving Breaker's World, so it was safe and sound during all the unpleasantness." Deetz was talking very fast now in the alien's native language; luckily Jason's translator kept him up to speed. "With the captain gone I had no way to get it back out of storage, so I enlisted this human," he gestured towards Jason, "to help me sign it out and bring it straight here. I know we're late, Bondrass, but you have to believe that I was trying to get here as soon as I could."

"I don't have to believe anything," Bondrass said with venom in his voice. He gestured to the two behind him. "Go check it out and let me know what you find." While he spoke he never took his eyes off the DL7 crew and seemed especially interested in Jason. The guards immediately jogged up the ramp and began scanning the barrels in the cargo bay with some sort of handheld device. Jason was captivated by the alien in front of him, but he had also seen Twingo's reaction when Deetz had called him by name. It was the same reaction Jason would have had if he had been hitchhiking and found himself standing in John Gotti's garage facing the Don himself with two of his goons behind him. For the first time since boarding the gunship in that clearing, Jason began to think that it wasn't likely he would actually survive this little adventure.

He was actually grateful when he heard the two armed beings marching back down the ramp, if for no other reason than to interrupt the uncomfortable silence between them and the imposing Bondrass. The pair went straight to their boss and one whispered quietly in his ear as he continued to stare blankly at the trio, his face belying no emotion. Suddenly, his face broke into a huge, oily smile, exposing his short, pointed teeth.

"It seems all is in order. I'll admit, I had my doubts." He walked over and put an arm around Jason and Deetz, the latter involuntarily flinching away slightly at the gesture. "But you understand that, don't you Deetz? After all, you guys disappeared with my cargo at the pickup and it's taken all this time for you to bring it back here. I half expected the containers to be full of sand." With gentle pressure Bondrass was leading them away from the ramp. "But now all is well and you've shown yourselves to be standup guys. We can maybe talk about some business later. Don't go anywhere." The last sentence was most definitely not a suggestion. The tall alien removed his arms and strode away towards the exit, his two guards falling into formation behind him.

Jason was slightly confused as a work crew seemed to materialize out of nowhere and began unloading the cargo hold using some sort of hovering sleds, and another alien, the same species as Bondrass apparently, albeit much shorter, appeared in front of him with a tablet computer. "As you'll see here, Bondrass has graciously agreed to pay ninety percent of the original contract, most generous considering how late you've been. If you'll please place your imprint here," he indicated to another highlighted circle on the screen. Jason looked to Deetz, who nodded almost imperceptibly, and pressed his thumb into the circle. The tablet beeped and the alien looked at the screen and frowned. "I've never heard of a … human? … interesting. No matter though, your bio print matches the ship's record, payment is being transferred to the DL7's treasury as we speak. Once the cargo is unloaded, you're free to reboard and grab your personal belongings. Bondrass has arranged for a suite to be made available for you and will notify you shortly if he has further use for you. If not, you'll be cleared to leave." The officious being spun around on his heels and marched out of the hangar, leaving

Twingo and Jason both apprehensive and relieved. Deetz, on the other hand, looked only relieved.

It took the crew another twenty minutes or so to clear out the gunship and spirit away the cargo. During that time, Jason walked over to lean against the nose landing gear and stare out of the gaping hangar opening into space. Intellectually he knew there was a forcefield holding the atmosphere in the hangar, but part of him was still quite leery of the hard vacuum that was just a few yards away. Once the ground crew left, he walked up the ramp and into the middle of an argument between Twingo and Deetz.

"This has nothing to do with me! I'm booking the first flight back home and YOU'RE going to pay for it!"

"You know exactly who that was out there. Do you really think he'd make the distinction between you wanting to be here or not? As far as he, and I, is concerned, *nobody* is leaving until he says otherwise. Believe me ... I'd like nothing better than to dump you right here and now. The fact you're on board was not my choice. The fact Bondrass has told all of us to stay, including you, is also not my choice." Deetz's voice remained calm, but the steel in his demeanor indicated that he meant to back up what he said.

"Look here, you chunk of scrap metal, I don't give a leap what you've got cooked up with whichever crime lord you're dumb enough to have dealings with. I'm not bound to any of it and I'm leaving!"

"ENOUGH!" Jason's shout froze both of them just as Deetz looked like he was winding up for another long-winded retort. "Deetz ... with the money this job paid, do you agree to send Twingo back to Breaker's World on the first available transport?" He waited for the synth to nod his assent. "Thank you. Twingo ... would you agree to this with the condition you wait for a bit to see what's what with this Bondrass character?

I know you'd rather leave, but I'd rather you not put us in danger, or mark yourself."

"Fine," Twingo said without conviction. Clearly he'd much rather be on the first flight away from Pinnacle, but he'd gotten all he was going to get out of the other two.

"Okay. That's settled. I suppose we can just grab what we need and head out. I'm guessing that little guy still waiting by the door is going to show us to our rooms." Jason didn't wait for a response as he headed back to his quarters to grab what few belongings he had to take with him: a change of clothes and the toiletries he'd managed to coax the fabricators into producing.

He almost had everything bundled into a neat roll with his change of pants on the outside when there was a soft knock at his door. He walked over and slapped the spot on the wall that would open it. Twingo was standing there with a similar bundle to his own. "May I come in, Jason?"

"Of course. Something wrong?"

"Honestly, yes … but I don't think you fully realize it yet." The engineer came in and sat down in the chair at the desk. "This Bondrass is a notoriously bad, bad guy. I don't get a good feeling about staying here any longer than necessary."

"I can agree with you there, but I honestly don't think we have much choice at this point. I know I'm a backworld rube to you, but I recognize a gangster when I see one. What do you think he wants with us?"

"I can't really imagine. My first instinct tells me he's going to want another job done, but he has to know that Deetz is more of a con artist and you, although trained as a soldier on your own world, are very much out of your element here. He could buy and sell a thousand of me so that's certainly not it," Twingo said, pausing as if he wanted to say more.

"Go on," Jason prompted.

"It may be the ship. While something like this bird isn't necessarily unobtainable, it is a bit of a rare mix of firepower and speed. It would certainly be worth getting rid of three nobodies for."

"Something tells me you're here because you have an idea on how to prevent that rather than to just give me a warning."

"Very perceptive," Twingo smiled. "I'd like to use your authority to put some locks in place on the ship's computer. Bondrass' people would correctly assume Deetz has been in command of the vessel, but when you were named First Officer you automatically outranked him as far as the computer was concerned. I'm not sure that he realized that when he gave you such a high rank. The locks, that only you can control, could be used as leverage for anyone who would want to take the ship, be that Bondrass or Deetz." The last part surprised Jason somewhat. He hadn't realized just how deep Twingo's distrust of Deetz was. While the synth was supremely annoying, and he shared some of those misgivings, he didn't think he would deliberately put them in danger or run out on them at this point.

"Okay, tell me what to do," Jason said as he sat down on the foot of the bed. Over the next five minutes, Twingo talked him through the commands he needed to give the computer to gain access to the security protocols and safeguard them so only he could rescind them. Once finished, they grabbed their gear and headed back towards the cargo bay where they found a very impatient synth waiting for them.

"Where have you two been? You only have one change of clothes to your names ..."

"What?" Jason asked as he walked by. "We have a schedule to meet or something?" Deetz rolled his eyes and activated the security lock up, unwittingly triggering Jason's new subroutine, and walked down the ramp before it could raise and lock.

The concierge, who had been waiting patiently by the hangar access hatch, led them through the bowels of the lower station, his impeccable clothes clashing with the grimy surroundings. They arrived at a set of lift doors and were ushered inside. They rode the lift further and further until even Deetz's brow shot up as they traversed into the extremely posh upper decks of Pinnacle Station. The doors finally opened and they walked out into an opulent passageway, still following the concierge until they reached an open hatchway. Walking inside, they were momentarily stunned by how well appointed their temporary quarters were. Jason was the first to speak: "We're being buttered up for something. This can't be cheap."

"This is one of many suites Mr. Bondrass keeps on retainer for clients who may be passing through." It was the first time the concierge had spoken since they had exited the hangar. "If there won't be anything else, sirs, I'll leave you now. If you're needed, someone will send for you." He spun and walked out, shutting the hatch behind him.

"Anyone want to bet that it's locked?" Twingo asked as he sprawled out on the sofa, obviously deciding that he might as well take advantage of a little luxury while he could. Jason walked around the suite and, as on the gunship, was struck at how familiar the furnishings and fixtures were. He said as much.

"Why has everything looked like it could have come from my planet? For that matter, why haven't the aliens I've met been all that exotic?"

"Aliens?" Deetz laughed at him. "Take a look around, you're the most alien being on this station right now." He laughed again, ignoring Jason's glare.

"There's a logical reason for that," Twingo spoke up. "For whatever reason, intelligent life seems to evolve along a certain few tracts, mostly. Warm-blooded creatures all tend to be bipedal with bilateral symmetry once they reach a certain level of evolution. Some have more appendages or specialized sensory organs, but we're all pretty similar, and as such we tend to congregate together. On some worlds, insectoid life becomes dominant, or prime, and those species tend to stick together as well. It's more out of a lack of communication ability than any real prejudice, although some of them are a fright to look at. There's simply no real common ground for us to meet on. Beings like us tend to be more individualistic while insectoid life is more hive-oriented with a strong group-think instinct." Twingo took a sip of something he had grabbed from the wet bar before continuing. It looked suspiciously like a beer bottle to Jason.

"There have been some pretty nasty wars between the two, but for eons there has been a steady peace between us in this part of the galaxy. Well, more or less. We don't really compete for the same resources and aren't motivated by the same factors, so we've learned it's better to just ignore each other. Of course, there are some truly bizarre folks out there, energy beings and what not, but you don't get to interact with them all that much if you stick to the established worlds and space lanes."—another sip—"Any other questions?"

"Is that a beer?"

"That's seriously your only question?"

"Yes."

"OK," Twingo chuckled, raising his free hand up in mock surrender. "Yes, the cooler is stocked with a few varieties of ales from a couple of different worlds. I'm sure it's similar to what you have on your planet. Fermenting sugars seems to be the first technological leap we all take together." Jason walked over to the bar, opened the cooler door, and peeked inside. Sure enough, there were familiar bottles lined up, a little smaller than a twelve-ounce bottle and with a different style cap, but beer bottles nonetheless. *It can't be all that bad out here if they have beer.*

Taking a long pull off the bottle, Jason tilted his head back and let the liquid play across his palate. If he closed his eyes and didn't think at it too closely, it really did taste eerily similar to a Harp Lager from Ireland back on Earth with a little more body to it and a slightly sweetish finish. He took another drink and let out a breath. "Ahh ... I really did need that," he said, hoping the work the ship's medical bay had done on him so he could eat would also work its magic with the alien brew.

A loud, keening screech startled Jason so badly he spilled some of the beer on his shirt. He wiped at it as he looked for the source of the odd noise. *What the hell ...* He spotted Twingo sitting at a computer terminal, his normally bluish hue now a sickly pallor. He looked so agitated that Jason walked over to see what the issue was. Unfortunately, he couldn't read a single word on the screen. What he could see, however, were the images, and one of the four on the screen was of the gunship in flight over Breaker's World, its main engines at full power. Another was of Twingo. It looked like a mug shot so Jason assumed it must have been a photo from his employer or an ID database.

"What's it say?" he asked, unable to hold back any longer.

"I'm wanted for questioning in the deaths of three individuals and the escape of a Jepsen Aero DL7 gunship," Twingo replied simply.

"Well that's ridiculous. You were an innocent bystander," Jason said, placating his friend. "That should be easy enough to clear up."

"You don't understand!" Twingo turned on him with an uncharacteristic ferocity. "Breaker's World is run by the cartels. They KNOW what happened, but they don't care. They want you guys and that ship, but all they have is a positive ID on me." He placed his head in his hands and started moaning. "I can't believe this." Jason didn't know what else to do, so he was surprised when Deetz came forward and placed a hand on Twingo's shoulder.

"Maybe you should try to go lay down for a bit and clear your head. This is obviously about the cargo we were carrying. We can have Bondrass' people clear this up with the local cartels on Breaker's World," the synth said with what seemed to be genuine concern for the little engineer. Twingo simply nodded and plodded off to one of the rooms without a word. Once the door closed, Deetz turned to Jason. "That's probably good advice for you too. I don't really know what's going on and I'd like to have you rested and alert when we find out." He looked pointedly at the half-empty bottle. "I'd really rather not have you intoxicated either."

"Probably not a bad idea," Jason agreed without argument. He left the bottle on the bar and headed towards one of the other empty rooms, intent on a shower and then some sleep.

Chapter 11

Jason awoke some time later, not knowing how long he had slept, to the sound of voices coming from the main room. One was clearly Deetz, and one was clearly not. He stayed still and concentrated, still unable to make out what was being said. "Son of a bitch," he murmured under his breath, grabbing the translator earpiece off the table next to the bed. He stuffed it into his right ear but by the time the little device had booted up, the other unidentified voice had left. Figuring there was no point in lying there any longer, he swung his legs off the bed and stood up, pulling on his shirt. After multiple combat tours he slept in his pants and boots when he was in an unknown or potentially hostile environment. This counted as both in his book.

When Jason walked out into the main living area he saw Deetz sitting at the computer terminal reading documents at breakneck speed. Twingo was nowhere in sight, likely still sleeping. Deetz looked over at him and gestured to the larger sofa. "A gift for you. From Bondrass, or more likely his consigliere. We're invited to dine with him in three hours."

"An invitation would indicate we have the option to turn it down," Jason said as he picked up what looked like two garment bags.

"A poor choice of words perhaps. I should have said in three hours we WILL be dining with Bondrass at his pleasure. I'm assuming there is something along the lines of a job he'd like us to undertake," Deetz replied as he turned back to the display. Jason was about to retort that he wasn't aware there was an "us" in the equation, but bit back the comment and walked to his room with the larger of the garment bags.

The clothing was fairly straightforward: pants, a shirt, and a banded-collar jacket that went high up his neck. It was actually more elegantly simple than an Earthly suit and tie. What he was amazed and suspicious about was the tailoring. The clothes fit him absolutely perfectly in every way: the neck, inseam, and even the fact that his left shoulder was minutely lower than his right. He assumed he must have been scanned at some point while walking through Pinnacle Station, something his human sensibilities took offense to for some reason.

He walked back out of his room a short time later to see that Twingo's door was still shut, but the other garment bag was missing. Deetz was sitting on the sofa watching what must have been a newscast on the largest display he had ever seen. Jason stared for a moment, trying to figure out why a machine would bother sitting on the sofa in the first place. He walked to the bar and grabbed another beer out of the cooler, ignoring the synth's reproachful gaze. *Screw him. If I'm being forced to go along with this I'm going to do it relaxed.* He hadn't felt any ill effects from the previous half a beer he had drank so now it was bottoms up. He apparently wasn't the only one with a case of nerves as Twingo, emerging from his room resplendent in his new suit, walked straight to the bar without comment and grabbed a bottle of something off the shelf above the counter and poured a liberal amount into a glass. He fired the drink back, winced, and then repeated the process twice more before speaking to his companions. "How much longer?"

"We've got about an hour and a half," Deetz said.

"Seeing as how we're obviously not being treated like prisoners, do we really need to wait around to be collected by an underling?" Jason set his empty bottle back on the bar and stared at Deetz.

"I'm not sure I follow you," he replied.

"What I mean is this: can't we go early and wait for our host? I'd sort of like to get a view of the place before I have Bondrass' people watching my every move."

"I know which establishment we're going to, so I suppose it's possible. We could wait in the lounge, I'm certain our movements will be monitored, but what you're suggesting may not be a bad idea." Deetz switched off the display and rose from the couch.

"So there's really no way I can just stay here?" Twingo paled visibly now that the meeting with the crime boss went from being a hypothetical event in the future to a reality in the present.

"You know the answer to that," Deetz said gently as he walked with Jason towards the door.

"Try and relax a bit, Twingo. If a few peons like us were simply going to be killed, I doubt we'd be getting dinner and gifts. Unless this Bondrass is one sick bastard," Jason said, looking at Deetz, who just shrugged noncommittally.

The restaurant they were heading to was three decks below them and along the outer edge of the hull, providing diners with spectacular starscapes as they ate. Nobody tried to stop them along their way, confirming that they were probably free to roam around the station somewhat without drawing the ire of Bondrass. They were seated at a table in the lounge and the two biological beings ordered drinks. All three settled in to watch the ebb and flow of the crowd and wait for their host.

The flurry of activity near the entrance was their first indication that the main event was about to kick off. Some oversized aliens of a species Jason had not yet seen led the way in, obviously point security by the way they scanned the crowd. A couple of underlings walked in and then Bondrass appeared, all smiles and waves to the crowd, his shimmering black suit complementing his olive green skin. He spotted the gunship crew and waved like they were old friends, making several patrons look at the trio with new interest.

"Boys!" he boomed. "Starting without me? Let's all grab another drink before we head to our table." While his demeanor was bombastic and friendly, Jason could see through the act. It was more for the benefit of the other patrons in the lounge than to put them at ease.

A short while after Bondrass' arrival, they were shown to their table. Only the boss and his right-hand man joined them; the rest of the entourage mingled around in the lounge or posted up discreetly at the entrance. Once they had all ordered (Jason with the help of Deetz), things turned to business.

"I don't always give my contractors the royal treatment like this," Bondrass started, taking a sip of what looked like a dark red wine. "But you've proven that you're able to overcome adversity and still remember who it is you work for. Frankly, I was surprised when you showed back up with my cargo completely intact. We've tested it and it wasn't tampered with in the least." Jason could tell they were on dangerous ground. He hoped Twingo would just keep his mouth shut and Deetz would find a graceful way to get them out of any future obligations to this guy. "What I was equally surprised at, Deetz, was the complete crew change. Not that I was especially partial to Klegsh, it was the ship I was hiring, but for a synth you've shown a remarkable self-preservation instinct and uncommonly good sense. No offense intended."

"None taken, sir, and I thank you for the compliment. Of course it goes without saying that it never crossed my mind to try and cross you," Deetz said. Bondrass looked unimpressed with the synth's bootlicking.

"Of course. Which brings me to the main point, as it were." Bondrass leaned back and took another drink. "I have an … opportunity … for you to make some serious cash for not a lot of work."

"I'm listening," Deetz said eagerly.

"I need some cargo and personnel moved fairly quickly from this station to another location, not on a planet. My ships are all too well known to be able to slip out of here without someone observing, but your vessel is virtually anonymous, save for that action on Breaker's World. You could get out of here with minimal effort and be done with the job within a matter of days, paid and on your way."

"That sounds extremely generous, sir. Do you think it'd be possible for me to discuss this with my crew and give you an answer?" Deetz's answer completely took Jason by surprise. He assumed that the synth would jump at the chance of another job and Jason and Twingo would be the ones trying to convince him to walk away. Something had changed and he didn't know what it was.

"I suppose," Bondrass said, shifting irritably in his seat. "You should know, I would like to use you and your … crew … again, but all I really need is the ship. A DL7 isn't that difficult to pilot." *There it is … the offer we can't refuse.*

"We'll take the job," Jason heard himself saying. Bondrass leaned back and smiled, Deetz looked at him sharply, and Twingo looked ready to faint.

"Well, Commander Burke, that makes me very happy," Bondrass said. "Smart move. Of course, your crew is only three people, not nearly enough to manage that big gunship. I'll tell you what I'll do … I'm going to provide some of my own personnel to make sure the delivery goes smoothly. It's the least I can do."

I'll bet.

Once back in the suite, Jason had to fend off two very irate beings. "Why the hell did you jump in back there?" Deetz seemed more upset that Jason had usurped his authority than at the prospect of working for Bondrass again.

"We were supposed to be getting out of here! I want to leave!" Twingo's reaction was fear-driven, and understandable. Jason was in no mood to coddle him though; he wanted to be done with this as much as anyone. He also wanted to be done with all the arguments about it.

"If you'd both shut the hell up, I'll tell you," Jason yelled, his tone renouncing any argument. "You both heard him … he said all he needed was the ship, that was a direct threat. He'll TAKE that gunship parked down in the hangar, and when he does, what do you think our life expectancy looks like? You think we'll be allowed to just run out the clock in this luxury suite on his dime? We'll be dead before they even finish loading the cargo." They stared at him silently, contemplating what he had just said.

"You're right," Twingo said softly. "We'll never be allowed to leave here alive unless we play his game." He blew his breath out noisily. "What do I care? I'm a wanted man on my home planet … which isn't even really my home planet. I've no one to care for, or to care for me, but I don't want to die here on this station. I guess I'm in for now."

"I don't disagree with you, but these things are usually handled with a little more finesse," Deetz conceded. "Since you've locked us into this deal without discussing terms, we're obligated to do this for whatever price he may set." Jason looked at him with disgust.

"Deetz, I'm not trying to get more money out of him. I'm trying to survive long enough to see Earth once more."

*****

The crew of the gunship was back down in the hangar deck bright and early, at least according to ship's time, watching the last of the cargo get moved up into the hold and secured. Towards the end of the loading, Bondrass made an appearance, looking as polished as ever. He was trailed by a handful of aliens that were dressed in utilitarian coveralls, almost like flightsuits, and were undoubtedly their "supplemental crew members."

"Looks like we're about ready," the crime boss beamed. "Let me introduce you to the specialist you'll be taking with you. This is Dr. Jorvren Ma'Fredich. He'll be monitoring the cargo and disembarking once you reach your destination." Jason nodded politely to the doctor, who looked like he may have been the same species as Twingo, and was rewarded with an openly hostile glare that startled him. "Are we about ready to launch?" Bondrass asked.

"Yes, once your personnel are on board we can shove off." Bondrass cocked his head slightly, as if trying to decipher the expression. After a split second his implants provided him with his species' equivalent of the nautical term, "shove off," and he smiled. "So how is it you're still using that old, cheap translator? Never mind." Cutting Jason off before he could answer, Bondrass motioned for one of his men. After a brief conversation he straightened back up and yelled at the doctor, "Ma'Fredich! I'm sending for a full set of implants for Commander Burke. You WILL use this ship's medical facilities and install them." The doctor looked positively enraged as he stared at Jason before stomping up the ramp. Bondrass chuckled. "Just a little parting gift for a job well done." As Jason watched him walk off he realized the implants weren't a gift, they were an insult aimed at the doctor. Apparently one of many, judging by the looks Ma'Fredich had been giving. Sighing, Jason turned and followed everyone else up the ramp and into the gunship.

The cargo bay was loaded with twenty-eight tall, rectangular modules that were individually secured to the deck. They looked to be about one and a half meters by one and a half meters and around four meters tall. All the containers were humming and had indicator panels that were scrolling information that Jason couldn't understand. He innocently asked the "hired help" next to him, "So what's in the crates?"

"Don't worry about it, and don't touch anything." The flight-suited thug pushed by him and headed for the stairs that led to the interior of the ship. When Jason left the cargo bay himself, waiting to watch the ramp raise and lock to prevent any potential stowaways, he walked into the ship and felt a completely different vibe to it. The personality (or lack thereof) of Bondrass' people aside, the ship didn't have the abandoned feel to it that he had gotten used to in recent weeks as the sole occupant.

The three new security thugs, as Jason came to think of them, were sitting at the galley table engrossed in a conversation amongst themselves. The doctor was sitting apart from them staring down into a mug of something. He looked as dejected as anyone Jason had ever seen. Before he could initiate a conversation with him, Deetz's voice came over the ship intercom: "We'll be launching in five minutes. There's no need to secure yourselves or other items since we'll just be sliding out of the hangar. Commander Burke, please report to the bridge."

"What's up?" Jason asked as he walked onto the bridge, nodding to Twingo as he passed.

"We're getting ready to launch. I'd rather have you up here in case our new passengers have a secondary agenda. We can close off the bridge if we need to and evacuate the atmosphere out of the rest of the ship if it looks like they're here for something other than just to tend to the cargo." Jason was somewhat surprised that the synth seemed to have real concern for his well-being.

"Thanks," he said simply as he hopped into the copilot's seat.

The DL7's reactor was still coming up to nominal operating range when Deetz went ahead and lifted off from the hangar deck and used the maneuvering thrusters to nudge the gunship out through the forcefield and into open space. Once out, he sat back as the station's docking control system took over navigation and flew the ship away, allowing the station's orbital velocity to aid in increasing the distance between the two. It was nearly five minutes later when the displays indicated that the ship was free-navigating and Deetz was clear to bring the main propulsion online. The ship thrummed as power was fed to the grav-emitters and they banked onto a course that would lead them directly out of the system. He began entering information into the navigation system and said idly to Jason, "We're going to make a couple of 'dummy jumps' in case we're tracked out of the system. Bondrass was right, this ship doesn't have much notoriety and has never been publicly contracted by him, so it's not likely anyone will follow. We'll jump once and then send the maintenance bots out to check the hull for trackers and then make a couple more hops before heading to our destination."

"Which is?" Jason asked.

"It doesn't really have a name. Everyone just calls it 'The Vault,' I think it's been intentionally left a bit ambiguous."

"I'm overwhelmed by the amount of detail you're giving me," Jason said sarcastically.

"Hmm? Oh," Deetz said distractedly. "It's an asteroid that has a decently stable orbit and is comprised mostly of iron ore. It was hollowed out for use as a deep-cold storage facility and was then repurposed as a sort of way-point for people who like to operate outside local jurisdictions."

"It sounds like just another space station with a natural hull. Isn't it the same as Pinnacle Station?"

"Oh no, Pinnacle Station is fully under control of both Pinnacle Prime and ConFed governments. Most of what you saw on that station was fully legal enterprise; it's a major shipping hub as well as a connection point for commercial spaceliners." Deetz activated the slip-drive and the DL7 disappeared from Pinnacle System's space.

Chapter 12

Each subsequent jump before they changed course to bear on their final destination was uneventful. Once they were steaming along towards The Vault, Jason climbed out of his seat and headed down to see what the passengers were up to. Twingo followed him out without a word. Dr. Ma'Fredich was in the infirmary and looked engrossed by something on one of the displays so Jason let him be. The trio of security goons had dispersed once they were in slip-space; two were in berthing, probably asleep, and one was sitting in the lounge. It seemed they were dividing into shifts in order to provide full coverage and ensure nobody would be molesting the cargo. Jason decided to ignore the lot of them and followed Twingo down into the engineering spaces. The pair walked into the main engineering bay and Twingo closed and secured the door. Jason looked at him with an arched eyebrow and waited for the engineer to say something.

"So, how confident are you that we're going to walk away from this?"

"Not as confident as I'd like to be," Jason admitted with a sigh. "I was mainly trying to escape Pinnacle Station and then try to get us home from there, but I didn't count on the added passengers."

"Once we reach The Vault we're going to need to try and find transport out of there. We can just leave the gunship and try to book passage to someplace safe. What is your planet ... Earth? ... What is it like?" Twingo apparently hadn't grasped the full meaning of Jason's story about how he came to be there.

"Um, it's nice ... but I don't think you want to go there unless you want to spend your remaining days in a cell. We've never had official contact with any species other than ourselves; if you showed up in a rented spaceship you'd cause a global panic."

"Oh, so you weren't exaggerating that part of your story, were you?" When Jason shook his head, he continued. "Well, that's out. Any other ideas?"

"Commander Burke, please come to the infirmary," the voice of Dr. Ma'Fredich over the intercom cut off Jason's reply. He looked at Twingo, who shrugged in return, and made his way up to the infirmary.

He walked into the ship's medical bay and was greeted by a glaring Dr. Ma'Fredich. "Sit," he said brusquely. Jason planted his feet and crossed his arms, staring flatly at the alien. After a few moments of rising tension the doctor caved, visibly deflating in defeat. "Sit on the table, please, Commander." Jason let it drop and hopped up on the table.

"Is this about something specific?" Jason asked. The doctor stared at him blankly for a moment.

"Implants, maybe?" he said, his voice dripping scorn and sarcasm as if this should have been completely obvious to Jason. "I've accessed your initial bio scans from the ship's computer. Quite fascinating really, I'd love to study your species in depth ..." He drifted off, lost in thought. Jason noticed that while he was studying the scrolling data he lost some of the brittle demeanor and became the curious scientist. "Anyway," he said, once again guardedly, "your physiology is imminently suitable for enhancement. You could actually have some extensive work done and hardly even notice it, but today it's just the usual workup: neural access implants, active translation matrix, and some processing enhancements to support those."

"I have no idea what any of that means," Jason admitted with trepidation. He was right on the verge of walking right out of the infirmary and telling the doc thanks, but no thanks. Ma'Fredich's face softened slightly as he saw how scared his patient was.

"Try to relax, you really won't feel a thing, and I'm going to put you out for the unpleasant part. These will also take some time to adapt and come online, so you won't notice a huge difference at first. Once you're accustomed to them you can begin to modify the interface." He turned and began pulling items out of the box that had been given to him by Bondrass' people. "So, how is it you're completely implant-free? In fact, I'm seeing some old injuries and other pathologies in your scan that look like they were healed naturally ... how is this even possible?" Jason avoided direct references to Earth and gave the doctor his story in broad strokes. As he talked he could sense the alien's demeanor towards him changing, becoming less combative.

"So, you're not one of Bondrass' hired thugs? Just someone in the wrong place at the wrong time?" Ma'Fredich seemed genuinely stunned.

"Something like that," Jason replied.

"Well, Commander Burke, it seems that this has been quite the adventure for you," the doctor chuckled. "Please, just relax and lay back on the table and we'll get started." Jason immediately drifted off to sleep as the sedative took hold. Once he was out, Dr. Ma'Fredich began the process of programming the nanites and injecting them into his bloodstream, carefully monitoring Jason's bio readout to ensure everything was going as it should.

Jason had no idea how long he'd been out, but he was sure that he must have been in a fight during that time; everything was sore and he felt majorly hungover. He squinted at the overhead light and realized he was still on the infirmary bed; what looked like an active full-body scan was showing on one of the displays that he could see from his position. His major systems were displayed along with vital information on each, although he couldn't read what it said. The door hissed open and he tried to look up to see who was entering, but he couldn't from the angle the bed was at.

"Well look who's coming back around!" Twingo's boisterous voice assaulted his ears. It sounded different somehow, but unmistakable.

"How do you feel, Jason?" Again, he recognized the voice of Dr. Ma'Fredich, but there was something different about it. He looked up as the two came along either side of the bed and looked down at him.

"I feel like smashed ass ..." The pair laughed immediately at that and the doctor pressed a hypospray against his arm and injected him with something that felt cool as it entered his bloodstream.

"This should help. I wanted to make certain everything was okay once you woke up before I gave you anything for the discomfort. You're the first human I've ever worked on, so better safe than sorry," Ma'Fredich said as he turned to the readout Jason had been observing earlier. Jason's eyes narrowed suspiciously. He'd never told the doctor his species. After a few nods and mumbles to himself, the doctor turned back to him. "Everything appears to be in order. How does the translator sound to you?" Jason realized at that point he was hearing their natural voices, and that was why they'd sounded differently to him; he was talking to them without the aid of the translator device that Twingo had originally given him.

"Sounds great, I didn't even notice the translator earpiece was gone until just now actually," Jason said. He marveled at the technology, but decided he didn't want to delve too deep into what it was doing to his brain to allow him to communicate with alien species fluently. "So what else is new in my head?"

"Well," Ma'Fredich began, looking at the info on a tablet computer, "the translator works, obviously. The primary neural implant is also working since that's what is allowing the translator to interface with your brain. Some other subsystems are still organizing themselves so we'll give them a little more time before we activate them. Your ocular display system looks almost ready to activate ..." As the doctor droned on Jason realized that he was relating to him in an entirely different way. When they had first met, the doctor had seemed openly hostile. It was as if Jason had given some great insult, but now there was almost a friendly quality to the interaction that was reinforced by the not-quite buddy-buddy vibe he was getting from him and Twingo. When he realized Ma'Fredich had stopped talking and was looking at him, he felt compelled to say something.

"Well, I feel okay now. Whatever you gave me must be kicking in." The doctor gave him an odd look, but hit the restraint release nonetheless.

"Okay, let's just take it easy then. We'll stop by the galley and then it's back to your quarters where we'll check up on you from time to time." The pair helped him into a sitting position.

"How long was I out?" Jason asked instead.

"About twelve hours," Twingo volunteered. "Not too bad really, I know when I got my first set I wasn't up and about for a day or two." Jason really did feel better as whatever the doctor had injected him with began to kick in. He put on the proffered hospital-style slippers with as much dignity as he could muster and shuffled out between the shorter doctor and engineer towards the galley.

Suddenly ravenous, Jason ate with gusto as his two friends chatted away and one of the ubiquitous security guards at the other end of the table tried to ignore them, occasionally throwing a glare their way after a particularly raucous bout of laughter. After his second helping, Jason felt himself growing sleepy and almost nodding off at the table as Twingo and Ma'Fredich prattled on like a couple of teenage girls. Looking more closely, he could see the doctor was very similar but obviously a different species than Twingo. The ears were the giveaway; Twingo's large expressive ears which fluttered to emphasize parts of his speech were smaller and passive on Ma'Fredich. The doctor also had a slighter build compared to the stocky engineer, as well as the same number of digits he himself had: five per hand. Jason did notice that Ma'Fredich did appear to be double jointed and could bend his fingers inward and backward. While it was interesting, it certainly wasn't enough to keep him awake.

"Well boys, I'm hitting the rack," he said as he pushed away from the table. "See you later."

"We're not going anywhere," Twingo said. Jason rolled his eyes and trudged off to his quarters for some sleep.

beep-beep

Jason rolled over, not quite awake, but not fully asleep.

beep-beep

This better be good ... He knew The Vault was still a few days away even with the incredible speed the DL7 was cruising at. He wanted nothing more than to sleep the "implant crud" off, but his door chime seemed to have other ideas. "Come in!" Jason shouted to the wall. The computer unlocked and slid the door open to reveal Twingo and Ma'Fredich standing in the passageway. The lights behind them were dimmed, indicating it was "night hours" on board. The pair slid in and managed to look a little sheepish as they saw Jason sprawled out on his bed, staring at them through heavy-lidded eyes.

"We need to talk." Ma'Fredich was the first to speak as they entered his quarters and slid the door shut. Twingo held up a finger to his lips.

"Computer, disable all auditory monitoring devices within these quarters," Twingo instructed the computer.

"Authorization needed," the emotionless tenor informed them. Twingo looked to Jason.

"Do it," he said.

"Acknowledged. Monitoring systems disabled in the captain's quarters under authorization of First Officer Commander Burke." The ship fell silent.

"I take it this isn't a social call," Jason said. The vibe in the room was heavy; whatever was on their minds had put them both in a somber mood. Twingo gestured to Ma'Fredich that he should do the talking.

"From what Twingo has told me, this isn't the type of work you guys normally do. I'm putting not an insignificant amount of trust in you by telling you this." He took a deep breath and stared at the ceiling for a moment before continuing. "Do you know what the containers in your cargo hold are? No? Well I'll tell you; they're stasis pods, designed to hold biological entities intact for long-term storage or movement. These are typically used for dangerous prisoners or medical patients. The pods in your hold contain neither; you've unwittingly been drawn into the trafficking of sentient beings against their will."

Jason's stomach tightened and performed a somersault at that last bit. He stared at the doctor in horror, not wanting to believe what he had been told. Ma'Fredich went on, "Before I continue, I suppose I should know what your views are on this practice."

"Some of our darkest chapters involved the enslaving of our fellow man. I can't overstate the revulsion most of us feel at this."

"Most?"

"Unfortunately, it does still exist even today," Jason said uncomfortably. "We're not a unified planet, and not all regions feel the same. There are some countries that still look the other way." As he said it out loud, he felt a profound sense of shame for the human species. He was painfully aware of his species' level of sophistication compared to many of the beings he'd met and was still a bit defensive about it.

"They really are a relatively young species," Twingo came to Jason's defense, making him feel all the worse for it.

"I see," the doctor continued. "Your homeworld and its internal politics aren't germane to this particular conversation. What are important are *your* views on the subject, of which you seem quite sincere. Twingo and I have been discussing some possible options we have, but we're going to need your help."

"You're going to try and free them." Jason wasn't asking, he was stating the obvious.

"You wouldn't? I need to reclaim my honor, Jason. It's all I have left."

"How did you get mixed up in this?" If he was going to stick his neck out, he needed to know his co-conspirators were on the level.

"I'm a geneticist by trade but I have a background in molecular biology, and even a smattering of surgical experience. I was approached by Bondrass some years ago to enhance some of his security personnel and find a way to circumvent the rules concerning bio-enhancements in a hand-to-hand combat sport he has a major stake in. I refused outright and let him see my disdain for the whole idea. Bondrass is not someone you insult, as I discovered." He seemed to be breaking down as he tried to finish his tale. "He took someone very close to me: my sister. He used her as leverage to get me to perform the tasks he wanted. It wasn't enough just to have my servitude, he wanted to break me ... and break me he did. While I toiled away, he made certain I knew all the horrors he had heaped upon my sister. If I attempted to break away, call the authorities, or rescue her ... she would be killed. My arrogance had cost her everything, and my cowardice made sure she never got it back."

"Doc, why are you deciding to take action now?" Jason's voice was gentle, but he felt he needed to convince the doctor to abandon any rash plans that would endanger his sibling and himself.

"Bondrass no longer has any hold over me. My sister finally succumbed to the constant abuse. His only leverage is to threaten my life directly ... so he has no leverage."

"I guess you'd better start from the beginning," Jason said, now fully awake.

Over the next hour and a half the doctor laid out what he knew of the operation. Most of the beings that were stored at, and shipped to, The Vault were to be of some use, either as payment or direct entertainment for Bondrass and a handful of other crime bosses that made up the cadre. Many were pitted against each other in a type of blood sport that sounded like a vicious version of mixed martial arts tournaments on Earth. Others were used as shock troops once the proper behavioral controls were put in place. There were also the usual mix of what one would expect: sex slaves, trophies, and leverage against those being extorted, like Dr. Ma'Fredich.

The stasis pods were all eventually transferred to The Vault as a staging area before being sent off to their final destination. The security was somewhat lax, according to the doctor, since nobody in their right mind would dare cross any of the powerful bosses that controlled The Vault, much less all of them at once. This didn't mean it was going to be easy, however. The Vault was usually heavily populated and, from what Jason was hearing, it was often a free-for-all of true wild west-style proportions. The three sat in the captain's quarters for a few more long hours hashing out the plan and using the station schematics the doctor had stored on his personal computer. They didn't want to risk that one of the goons on board had the ability to monitor their use of coms and data networks, so they stayed off the main computer. Once they felt they had it down, Jason leaned back on his bed and laced his fingers behind his head, staring from one of his companions to the other. There was a long, heavy pause before he spoke.

"You know we're probably going to be killed for this, right?" Jason felt he needed to cut right to the heart of the matter.

"It's a good plan, Jason," Twingo protested. "Your species is quite adept at subterfuge, it seems."

"It's only a good plan because it's based on nothing. Doc's the only one who's been to The Vault, and even he admits he wasn't as observant as he should have been. If there's one thing in covert ops I've learned as a constant, it's that no plan survives first contact. This is likely to go sideways on us almost immediately."

"So you would rather not be a part of this," Ma'Fredich stated flatly, but without rancor. Jason stared at the ceiling a moment before blowing out a huge breath through pursed lips, startling the two others.

"No," Jason said, "I just want you both to understand exactly what the consequences of our failure will be. Or our success. Getting caught on the station is easy, we'll probably just get burned down and that'll be it. If we manage to pull this off *and* get away …" He shook his head, "I might be able to get back to Earth and hide, but you two will be marked men. Beings. Whatever."

"We've thought that through," Twingo said. "After learning what I have … I'm not sure how comfortable I'd be just walking away. It's easy to turn a blind eye to those you don't know and don't see, but we're hauling a load of them to what amounts to a life of anguish and torture. That makes each of us culpable in some way or another." Jason could only nod his agreement at the engineer's point of view. He reflected quietly for a moment, and then his eyes snapped wide open.

"Where the fuck has Deetz been during this flight? He hasn't been on the bridge for the entire time, I've checked."

"While you've been getting your implants and recovering, he's locked himself in the com room for much of that time," Ma'Fredich said.

"I'm not sure I like that he's being so secretive. He's the one loose thread in this plan; he wants this deal to happen, so it's likely he'll be a hindrance more than anything." Jason still didn't fully trust the sardonic synth.

"You know, we can find out what he's up to." Twingo was looking speculatively at the others. "It might not be such a bad idea to see who he's been talking to, and what about." He laid out what commands Jason needed to give the ship's computer to gain access to the com logs. Deetz had made an oversight when he named Jason as First Officer. He hadn't realized that as far as the ship was concerned, Jason was the de facto commanding officer in the absence of a captain, far outranking the administrative assistant who only spoke for the captain on certain matters. Either way, the first officer had access and privileges to nearly all parts of the ship, something Deetz probably hadn't expected Jason to discover on his own.

"Shit. Here are the com logs. The date and times are recorded but he deleted the message bodies," Jason said, dismayed. "The fact he bothered deleting the logs indicates whatever he's up to isn't something he wants us finding out about."

"That's true. I wouldn't be surprised if—"

"He's going active now!" Ma'Fredich was pointing to the new entry to the com log that had a flashing **ACTIVE** next to it.

"Computer, display active com traffic to this terminal and record," Jason said as he leapt off the bed and rushed to stand over Twingo's shoulder to look at the display. One of the monitors divided into two sections: one showed Deetz quite clearly, the other showed Bondrass in far less resolution. The crime boss was talking.

"… is going well on your end. I'm trusting you with some high value cargo this time."

"Everything is still on track, sir." Deetz's tone was servile and made Jason cringe in disgust.

"And what about our side deal?" Bondrass leaned into the camera so it appeared to zoom in on his face.

"I think we're a go on that. He's had his implants installed and has been recovering in his room. The engineer has been puttering around with the ship and the doctor seems to do whatever he can to avoid your men."

"Excellent. Once you land, incapacitate the human and have him put in stasis. I was going to have my men deal with the good doctor, but I think I want you to do it. Kill that arrogant, pretentious Ma'Fredich and I'll know you're my guy." Jason and Ma'Fredich looked at each other in alarm.

"What about the engineer?"

"Who cares? They're a dime a dozen, I'm sure someone in The Vault can find an interesting use for him. Who knows ... it may even actually be as an engineer." Bondrass' coarse laugh afterwards paled Twingo's normally blue hue. The crime boss continued, "Once that's done, and you've given the cargo to the handlers, get your ass back here with that beautiful ship. Klegsh may have been unwilling to sell her, but I can see you're much more reasonable. Bring that gunship back and you'll have earned a spot on my staff."

"That sounds excellent, sir. We're currently three days' flight out from The Vault. I'll contact you when everything is in order." The display blanked and a text header showing the log file location, time stamp, and message duration was displayed in its place. Nobody spoke for a long while.

"Well, I guess that settles what the bastard was up to," Jason broke the silence. "This changes the plan. We're going to have to neutralize Deetz *before* we hit The Vault."

"I can help with that," Ma'Fredich said. "I've got detailed files on the different types of synths, I'll work out a way to incapacitate him."

"I'll help," Twingo said. "I never did trust that damn machine, I knew he had to be working another angle after Jason told me his story. You sure we shouldn't just kill him?"

"Not yet," Jason said firmly. "This plan just became a lot more fluid, I may need him available still. If we blast him I won't have that option." Both nodded respectfully, indicating their assent. "Okay, so we know what we're doing in the short term. Doc, find a way to knock that backstabbing robot out. Twingo, I'll meet you in Engineering later to see about fabricating some concealable handheld weapons. I'd search the armory, but we need to be discreet. Any questions? No? Great. Now if you don't mind, I'm going to try and get a couple more hours of sleep." The two others took the hint and walked to the door. Ma'Fredich paused in the entryway and turned back to Jason.

"Jason, sometimes you call me 'Doc.' Is there some significance to this?

"Ah," Jason said, smiling. "It's short for doctor. In my time in one of Earth's military branches, my team always had a medic with us that looked after us. We all just called them 'Doc.' It's meant as a sign of respect, but if it bothers you I'll try to stop."

"No, no. I think I quite like it," Ma'Fredich smiled as he walked out the door. "Doc," he repeated to himself before the hatch closed completely. Jason smiled and shook his head before lying back down and trying to get some more sleep with all the dangers that surrounded him swirling through his dreams.

Chapter 13

Jason woke up only a few hours after his two friends had left his room. He felt refreshed and ready to get started nonetheless. Despite the seriousness and the danger involved with this latest mission, he felt completely exhilarated. After a shower and some breakfast he wandered down to Engineering. He wasn't surprised to see Ma'Fredich and Twingo together, standing by a work bench going over some type of schematic. The two had become nearly inseparable on this flight despite their differences in social standing and vocational backgrounds. The two saw him and waved him over to the table. From what he could tell, they'd been working tirelessly on their plan to knock Deetz out of commission.

"Fill me in, boys," Jason said, his usual chroot mug grasped firmly in his hand. They did. Although he didn't understand most of the technical aspects of the plan (or any of them, if he was honest) he took it on faith that the doctor and engineer could come up with a working plan. It was relatively simple on the surface, and in the end he had them fabricate three sets of the specialized equipment they would need to execute the plan; that way any one of them could get to the synth in case he acted before they did.

Next came the handheld weapons; they needed something like a hold-out pistol that couldn't be detected by the security scanners that may be in place in The Vault. Twingo had decided to go low-tech, in a way. "I took some inspiration from your weapon that was in the armory, Jason. Fairly archaic, but effective. While making an Earth-type projectile gun is plausible, the necessity for metals means it still may be detected." Twingo was showing an exploded view of what looked like a Buck Rogers version of an over-under Derringer pistol. "This baby is all synthetic and has no power source, that's the beauty of it. When you pull the trigger, a chemical reaction instantaneously generates the power to fire a single shot. The shot will destroy the emitter and consume the chemicals so I'm including two shots per weapon. It isn't much, I'll admit."

"No, it's perfect," Jason disagreed. "If it takes more than two shots with one of these, we've already fucked the entire operation up beyond repair. I love it. Build it." He nodded to the pair and left the engineering bay. He would have liked to have stayed to help out, but he would best serve their mission by wandering the ship and keeping Deetz and the guards distracted from what the other two were doing. With that in mind, he veered from his original course heading to the bridge and walked to the galley instead.

As Jason had hoped, one of Bondrass' security troops was seated at the table, as usual. He had no idea which one; the trio looked too similar and had the same apparent lack of anything that could remotely be considered a personality. He got another mug of chroot and sat directly across from the guard, plastering a wide, ridiculous smile on his face. "Hi!"

"What do you want?"

"I just realized that we've never really had a chance to talk, just you and me." Jason kept up the same stupid smile while the alien had a look on his face that said he'd rather scrape Jason off the bottom of his boot than talk to him. Wordlessly, the guard stood, glared at him, and stalked out of the galley area. Jason got up and followed him to the lounge. "Ah! Good idea, the seats in there are so uncomfortable. This will be much nicer." This time the alien actually snarled in disgust and stormed off toward crew berthing. As soon as he was out of sight the smile disappeared from Jason's face and was replaced with a scowl. His harassment paid off as two of the guards were out of the way for a while and the third wouldn't be leaving the cargo bay. He eyed the stairs to the upper command deck speculatively. It would be useful to go up and keep Deetz distracted, but he was afraid he wouldn't be able to keep up the charade of the ignorant rube, or be able to keep his hostility in check. He decided that Deetz would probably be just as interested in avoiding them and would likely stay on the bridge for the rest of the flight, so instead he turned and walked back to his quarters to go through the technical data Doc had left him on his new implants.

Nearly forty-eight hours later, Jason, Twingo, and Ma'Fredich had everything prepared that they would need to execute their plan. Since there was nothing to do but wait during the remainder of the flight, Jason took extra care to keep the nerves of his cohorts under control; they had never been in combat before, so they didn't know how to channel the stress and energy that came with a pending operation into something positive, or at least non-destructive. The easiest way he knew how to accomplish this was to make them do something genuinely useful. They were both too smart to be coddled. So instead of busy-work, he asked them to help him get his implants configured and tweaked to suit him. Afterwards, he was able to have pertinent information fed directly into his visual cortex. The displays appeared to float in his field of view in a way that seemed almost natural. Twingo even slaved the targeting system from his railgun to his neural interface. He could now engage targets without having to shoulder the weapon and sight directly through the optics. Jason's human brain seemed to adapt quickly and he soon developed an insatiable desire to see what other tricks his new wetware could do, but Doc cautioned him to take it easy and acclimate slowly. It was easy to become enamored with what the technology could offer to the point of becoming completely distracted and detached from reality, something they couldn't afford during the upcoming mission.

For his own part, Jason had to prepare himself for what was coming as well. He knew the likelihood of them pulling this off without any bloodshed was nonexistent, and although he was technically the only member of the team with military training, he had rarely directly taken a life. His time in the Air Force had been spent as a Pararescue operator, or PJ. While highly trained members of the special operations community, very rarely were they called upon as a tactical asset. Their job was to get into impossible spots, rescue and render aid to others, and egress. He had performed joint ops with SEALs and Marine Force Recon units, so it wasn't that he was squeamish, but after years of fighting in the Global War on Terror, he was weary of the constant fighting. That was the main reason he had been hiding in his family cabin high in the mountains. This time he knew he had no choice, though. The stakes were his very freedom and likely his life. So, in the end, the choice was quite simple: fight for freedom or live and die a slave. Or worse. It wasn't the potential for violence that bothered him. It was the fact that if he hadn't heard Deetz offering to give him up, he wasn't sure he'd be as inclined to get involved, and he didn't like what that said about him.

Chapter 14

The big day had arrived. They would be making their final approach to The Vault within the next eight hours and Jason could tell his team was pumped up on stress and stimulants. Timing would be critical, so he did everything he could to keep them settled down and made sure they ate a large meal and had plenty of sleep. His years in the field had taught him you ate and slept whenever, wherever you could during operations; there was no guarantee when you'd get another opportunity. He sat pensively on the bridge with Deetz as the synth guided the ship towards their target after emerging from slip-space. So far as Jason could tell, he suspected nothing.

They were almost on final approach before Jason could even tell which asteroid it was that they were heading for, and even then it was only because the ship highlighted it for him in his optical implants. The DL7 passed easily through a natural-looking tunnel that could have accommodated a much larger ship and slowed to a stop before what appeared to be a dead end. Jason's pulse quickened at this unexpected turn of events. Deetz turned to him and smiled mirthlessly. As he was about to inquire as to what was going on, Deetz cycled the landing gear down and a set of flood lights came on within the tunnel, illuminating a landing apron that had been hewn out of the tough iron ore of the asteroid. Beyond that were a set of massive blast doors that presumably led into the hangar deck. "Getting into this place is a bit of a trick. It may be notorious, but it's still a closely guarded secret," Deetz said as the gunship settled onto the landing pad. "This is actually a secure backdoor, if you will. If I hadn't transmitted the proper clearance codes we got from Bondrass, we would have been incinerated while still in the tunnel before we even saw the hangar door. The main dock, and entrance, are on the adjacent face of the asteroid and have much more prominent security protocols." Jason felt a small bit of elation at Deetz's description of their entry method; Doc had said they would likely enter through a hangar that bypassed the major bulk of security on the station. The security was more focused on controlling those visiting for the entertainment, not so much those that were there on official business.

After another series of com messages, a crack appeared in the blast doors and slowly they rolled apart. Jason could see another set of equally impressive doors that split and opened vertically behind that, creating a double-layered door that looked nearly impenetrable. It would be insanely difficult to enter The Vault through this port if you weren't invited. Once the doors were open, the gunship taxied forward and followed the go-to directions on their displays that guided them to the docking berth they had been assigned. After the ship stopped and leveled itself on its landing gear, Deetz began shutting down the primary flight systems, completely preoccupied. Jason rose and walked around to the pilot's seat. "We all set?"

"It appears so, I guess we should go tell the ..." Deetz never finished his sentence as Jason patted him on the shoulder, the seemingly friendly gesture eliciting an explosion of sparks. Deetz's voice scrambled and he stiffened in the seat. Trying to rise, he reminded of Jason of a stroke victim. The synth jerkily tried to come at Jason, who easily backed out of reach, a small device with two protruding electrodes in his right hand. A look of comprehension crossed Deetz's face before it froze completely and he collapsed in a heap.

"Twingo, get in here!" Jason called out. The engineer, who had been waiting in the port-side meeting room that was just aft of the bridge, raced in with his hands full of tools. He quickly flipped Deetz over and began cutting an access opening into his skin. Once through, he fiddled around inside and then installed the device he'd been carrying into the synth. He flipped Deetz back over and looked up, breathing hard and with his hands on his knees.

"That'll do it. I've interrupted his main power distribution center. If we have to, we can start individual subsystems without bringing him fully back online."

"Okay, let's get him down to Engineering and restrained. Bondrass' people in the cargo hold with Doc?" When Twingo nodded, they dragged Deetz off the bridge and threw him up onto a waiting cart. They whisked him off to Engineering as quickly as they could so as to not risk any of the three security personnel seeing them. After securing the unconscious mechanical being to a purpose-built chair, complete with heavy manacles, they looked at each other. "This is it. You ready?" Jason asked, satisfied with the calm nod he received in response.

Jason quickly donned his armor and grabbed their new hold-out weapons. Without a word, he and Twingo headed into the armory and brought up a live feed of the cargo bay on one of the terminals. Doc was talking to the three goons as he checked all the stasis pods. "Can never be too careful, you know. These units are great for what they are, but running on the internal systems for such a long flight is risky. Don't want the boss' cargo damaged before delivery ..."

"Computer, highlight the three passengers in the cargo hold that are not Dr. Ma'Fredich," Jason said. Instantly three pulsing green boxes appeared around Bondrass' men. "Now target them with the stunners." The boxes now pulsed quicker and changed to red. "Fire." A bright flash washed out the video feed and an instant later Doc was standing in the cargo bay surrounded by three unconscious goons. He looked up into the camera and smiled. Jason smiled also as he opened the blast doors that led from the armory into the cargo hold.

"Just in time, I'm not sure how much longer I could have kept them from opening the doors," Doc said as he accepted one of the hold-out guns from Jason.

"You doubting me already?" Jason asked with a laugh. "Computer, bring up the external aft video feed." The trio crowded around the display by the rear cargo hatch and saw there were four more hired goons milling about, looking bored. Jason smiled grimly and hit the controls to drop the ramp and open the interior pressure doors. "You're on, Doc."

"I need help up here!" Doc shouted from the top of the ramp. "Something's happened!" The four guards ran up the ramp and entered the ship just as Jason and Twingo slipped out of sight around one of the stasis pods.

"What's happening in here?" one of the goons asked, trying to establish himself as in charge.

"I don't know," Doc was saying, "they were checking the pods and there was a flash. When I came over they were like this. They appear to have been shocked. I didn't know what to do." Jason snuck back around and activated the internal pressure doors, leaving the ramp lowered. As the doors slid closed the four newcomers spun as one.

"Computer, stun the four new passengers that just boarded," Jason barked. As before, a bright flash, and then they had a total of seven knocked-out thugs. As he walked over he said to Doc, "I didn't know what to do?" He laughed as he repeated Doc's adlibbed performance.

"What?"

"Don't they know you as a doctor?" Jason was still laughing.

"Oh. Yeah." Doc managed to look sheepish as he began working the controls on one of the stasis pods.

"How're we doing?" Jason asked over his shoulder as he walked back into the armory.

"Good. Very good, actually. Nobody's going to bother checking on this ship and I doubt anyone is going to miss these miscreants."

"Excellent. Keep an eye on things anyway, Twingo." Jason had to shout to be heard through the open armory door.

"Already on it," came the muffled reply. Jason nodded in approval at how his

team had performed thus far; no panic and everyone rockin' and rollin' according to the plan. He enjoyed it while he could. Once in the armory, he opened one of the wall lockers and stepped back to look over a wide assortment of handheld weaponry. As his eyes lingered over each, his neural implant fed him the pertinent information on that particular unit. He decided on a short, shoulder-fired plasma carbine. It would get the job done without destroying the inside of the ship if he had to fire it. He hefted the weapon with a grin playing across his features. As a long time gun-geek, the smorgasbord of exotic weaponry available in the gunship's armory was almost intoxicating. When his life wasn't in danger he would love to find some quiet, out of the way corner of some world for some trigger time with each.

After charging and activating the plasma rifle, Jason walked back out into the cargo bay with the weapon leaned casually over his shoulder. He found his two friends working diligently on the stasis pods that had been singled out after a quick manifest search. "We sure we have the right guys? I'd hate to turn loose some maniac in here," he said.

"Yes, we're sure," Doc said in a pained voice. "These aren't violent criminals, although some of them could do a lot of damage and are likely not very happy right now," he conceded.

"We're waking up the technical guys now, although we're going to be three pods short so we're also bringing out some that will need to be restrained for the duration of the mission," Twingo added as he monitored the display on one of the pods. Jason left them to their work. They were already committed to the plan, so second guessing things at this point would be counterproductive. After about thirty more minutes of frenzied activity from the two, Jason began hearing the *pop-hiss* of the stasis pods opening. Unable to contain his curiosity, he moved over to look into one of them.

Another bipedal being was strapped tightly against a vertical, metallic gurney with a myriad of intravenous tubes running to different parts of its body. It also wore a snug breathing mask and was slight of build. What really caught Jason's eye, however, was the fact this alien had four arms; two larger appendages that sprouted from shoulders like he was used to, and two smaller, thinner arms that emerged from around the mid-abdomen area. When relaxed, the smaller arms tucked up in a way that reminded Jason of a praying mantis. This being had an especially large cranium that came down to a wide but delicate-looking jaw.

Hearing some more noises, Jason looked over to see that Twingo and Doc had removed three aliens from their stasis pods and had them lying down on the floor. The trio of newcomers were coughing and writhing around in apparent pain as Doc checked each of them over. When the pod he was standing in front of beeped he had to hustle out of the way as his friends rushed over to start pulling out the strange being he had been looking at.

"He's looking good. That's four for four," Doc murmured.

"Hopefully our luck keeps up," Twingo said. Jason was starting to get the hint that being stored in one of these upright coffins didn't always mean you were coming back out alive. That fact only solidified his resolve for what he knew was coming up.

"Jason! You may need to give us a hand with this guy … bring your gun." Doc was staring into another open pod as the four recently released prisoners started to sit up and lean back against their pods. Jason jogged over and nearly fell down from the double-take he did when he laid eyes on their fifth almost-liberated prisoner. He was enormous. He had to be every bit of seven feet tall and had to bunch up his massive shoulders to fit width-wise in the pod. The heavy musculature writhed and strained under the dark, almost black skin. He sported a bony crest that started at his brow and ran up the length of his forehead before disappearing into what Jason would have sworn were dreadlocks. Or he would have if they weren't moving, seemingly of their own accord. "I wasn't aware he was going to be on this load, but he's already awake so you'll have to deal with him."

The alien had a broad face with a short, lupine muzzle that looked to be full of large, sharp teeth. His intense, yellow eyes stared balefully at Jason and the plasma rifle the human kept half-trained on him. "What, exactly, did you want *me* to do?" Jason whispered to Doc.

"Talk to him," Doc said out of the corner of his mouth. "He's a part of the warrior class from a world with a specific caste system. He knows I'm not a soldier, but he might respect you as a fellow combatant." Jason was highly dubious of that. He also didn't doubt that the terrifying alien had heard every word they had been saying.

"Hey there, big guy," Jason said in what he hoped was his most charming, disarming voice. "Everything going okay for you?"

"Let me out and I will show you," the beast's voice rumbled out of his chest. Jason's eyes were fixated on his mouth as he talked. Even with the translation he could tell the alien had to practically chew his words in a mouth that looked more suited for shredding than articulating.

"We'll hold off on that for a bit. You have a name?"

"Crusher."

"Is that a family name?" Jason regretted the sarcastic remark even as it left his lips. Crusher's roar was deafening and he threw himself against the restraints, managing to rock the stasis pod as the wide straps holding him groaned in protest.

"Whoa! Whoa! Whoa! Take it easy!" Jason raised the weapon, trying to head off what looked to be a pending disaster.

"You capture me, torture me, confine me, and then you DARE to insult me?! Know this: I will NEVER submit!!" Crusher's bellowing roar was seriously testing Jason's control over his bladder. "Do with me as you will, but one day in the future you will turn your back on me, and it will be the last thing you ever do," the giant, angry alien finished in a grating whisper. Jason swallowed hard, trying to regain his composure. He noticed Twingo was trembling violently and Doc was quite pale. He also saw the other freed prisoners were hiding amongst the other pods.

"Well, Crusher," Jason began when he thought he had steadied his nerves enough to speak, "I'm hoping you'll reconsider that. You see, I'm not the guy who bought you. I'm the guy who's going to free you. This is a jailbreak." A look of bewilderment came over Crusher's brutish face as he stared at Jason and then over to Doc.

"That's right," Doc confirmed. "We're here to set you, and the others, free."

"Why would you do this?" The distrust was evident in Crusher's voice.

"Because we are," Jason cut off Doc's answer, not wanting to get into a protracted debate on the issue. "But we're not free and clear yet. We're actually on a ship inside The Vault right now in the middle of the operation. We could use some help." He didn't come right out and ask. He sensed it would be better for Crusher to volunteer than for him to try and coerce him through guilt.

"I will help," he said simply, his eyes never leaving Jason's. The human turned and cocked an eyebrow in Doc's direction, the question unspoken: *Can we trust him?* Doc nodded once and walked over to the pod and entered the commands to release the restraints.

Unlike the others, who had needed a while to recover from being in their stasis pod, Crusher hopped out of the machine and landed on the cargo bay deck with a resounding thud. Once he was standing in the open and able to straighten up, Jason marveled at the alien's powerful build. Crusher looked around the cargo bay and then towards the rear door. "What do you need me to do?" he asked.

"For now just keep watch back by the door ..." Jason didn't finish his sentence before Crusher deftly snatched the plasma rifle right out of his hands and strode off towards the rear doors and the video monitor that still displayed the view from behind the ship, taking up a defensive watch.

"Relax, his kind are incapable of duplicity. Once he says he's with us, he'll fight to the death to accomplish his mission." Doc had slid up next to him and also observed the lone sentinel at the rear of the ship. "We're about ready back here," Doc continued. "This is where it gets dangerous." When Jason simply nodded, the doctor walked back over and continued prepping the team. Jason watched as they loaded the still-unconscious guards into the now-empty pods and restrained them. It was almost time to see if they would be leaving here as free beings, or die trying.

"Everybody, gather around!" Twingo shouted after another fifteen minutes of activity. Once they were all in a loose huddle by the rear doors, he continued, "We're going to lay out the rest of the plan. It's fairly simple, but let's all make sure we understand." Jason looked up and noticed that Twingo was staring at him expectantly. He then turned and noticed everyone was looking at him as well.

"Commander ... the plan," Doc prompted. Jason stepped forward, accepting that he was technically the highest ranking member of the crew, and the responsibility that came with it.

"Right," Jason began. "You may have noticed that only seven of you have been released so far. That's for a reason; four of you are essential to the operation, you other three were let out so we could use your pods. What we're going to do, however, is get all of us out of here." Over the next few minutes Jason laid out the details of their operation and what was expected from key players. Everyone watched him with rapt attention and nobody seemed to be hesitant. They all knew what was at stake.

"So that's it, in a nut shell. I need one of the pilots to stay behind here and the other two pilots and the hacker to get ready to leave with us," he concluded his brief.

"Hacker?!" The voice was indignant and unsurprisingly high-pitched considering the source: the small, four-armed alien. "That's a rather crude term to describe what I do."

"I meant no offense, that's what we call those in your profession on my world" Jason offered. "What is your name?"

"You couldn't possibly pronounce it correctly," the offended little alien said loftily. "You can just call me Kage."

"Fine," Jason said impatiently. "So if not a hacker, what do you call what it is you do?"

"I'm a code slicer, the very best. I'm a Veran, we're naturally suited for this type of work."

"Very well, then. As I was saying," Jason continued, "one pilot here with the gunship, two pilots and the slicer with us, and the others will hang back here." He caught something in the eye of the pilot that was staying behind that he didn't like. Never one to ignore a gut feeling, he motioned Crusher to follow him away from the group.

"Yes?" the fierce alien asked.

"I'm not sure how much I trust the pilot that's staying behind here, but he's all we have, unfortunately."

"You think he may decide to just take this ship and leave once you're out of sight?" Crusher asked.

"That's crossed my mind," Jason admitted. "It may be nothing, it's just a hunch, but I'd like you to stay here and keep an eye on him. Either we're all leaving this rock together, or none of us are. No man left behind."

"Most commendable," Crusher rumbled with a nod of approval. "As to your problem, a warrior never ignores hunches. Not one that wishes to live very long, anyway. I will keep an eye on our shifty pilot, Commander."

"Excellent. Go ahead and keep that plasma rifle, not that I think you'd need it." Crusher smiled widely at that, or at least Jason hoped it was a smile. The giant let out a sharp, barking laugh and slapped Jason on the back, nearly sending him sprawling across the deck. He left Crusher and walked up to Doc, who was standing apart and fidgeting. "You going to be able to do this?"

"I must. So yes, I'll be ready to do my part," Doc said without much conviction.

"Okay, then. Let's do it." Jason turned to the rest of the crew, "Alright! We're a go!" He walked over and opened the rear doors and strode down the ramp with Doc. The pair walked casually across the hangar floor towards a cordoned-off area that looked like it had all manner of moving equipment. A violet-skinned being with a crested tuft of what appeared to be feathers waved familiarly to Doc as they walked by, not giving them a second glance. Jason breathed a sigh of relief as his confidence in their ability to succeed went up half a notch. "Friend?"

"Not particularly," Doc glared at him. "But I have been here a handful of times as part of my indentured servitude to Bondrass."

"Not picking a fight, Doc. Just trying to keep up an appearance of casual indifference," Jason said as they reached the corral holding the equipment. Doc walked up to a terminal, entered a numeric PIN, and then selected two lowboy-style anti-grav carts. They grabbed them and moved with purpose back to the ship and up the ramp. Twingo closed the inner doors as soon as they cleared the threshold.

Utilizing the cargo bay's gantry crane, they loaded four stasis pods onto each cart. Whatever mechanism was keeping the carts off the deck whined as the weight of the pods was added. Jason looked around and took a deep, cleansing breath. "This is it," he said. "Any last minute questions or concerns?" When nobody spoke up, he began pushing one of the carts towards the door as one of the pilots going with them pushed the other behind him. Doc was point man in front and Twingo, as well as the other two members of the team, walked between the two loaded carts. With a meaningful nod to Crusher, Jason departed the gunship. The hover carts' whine deepened when they automatically kept level in relation to the hangar floor as they descended the ramp.

Nobody gave them a second look as the crossed the vast hangar area, moving towards a large, well-lit archway that was teeming with heavily-armed security personnel. The one in charge nodded to Doc as they approached.

"You know the drill, Doctor."

"Of ... of ... of course," Doc stammered as he walked over to the scanner. Jason cringed on the inside. *Hold it together, Doc.* If the guard noticed the doctor's discomfort he didn't let on. All six of the crew moved through the scanner and, to Jason's elation, didn't set off any alarms with the hold-out weapons Twingo had designed. He took this as a good omen. Three other security guards worked hand-held scanners over the stasis pods. After a couple of minutes, they waved the crew back over to reclaim the carts, apparently satisfied that nothing dangerous was entering the station.

"All just formality, Doctor. You good making your way down to storage?"

"I am indeed. Thank you," Doc said, waving the crew forward. They hustled out of the security area and bore left into a dimly lit passageway. Jason looked to the right through another security archway—this one much more heavily fortified—and caught a glimpse of a raucous promenade that was lined with store fronts and bustling with quite a few different species of aliens before they were fully into the passageway.

They picked up the pace to a brisk walk that took them deeper into the station. Jason's neural implant gave him a warning that he was no longer in contact with the ship's computer as the iron ore that comprised the asteroid blocked the signal. After a few hundred meters more they came to a set of formidable-looking blast doors that were flanked by two heavily-armed, and armored, guards, both in red uniforms. This pair looked like real professionals, not like the others at the entrance to the hangar. These guys were protecting something of real value and the bosses were taking few chances.

The one on the right approached Doc silently and stood in front of him, looking at the crew and then at the stasis pods. Without a word, he looked back at Doc, seeming to be waiting on something. Jason's adrenaline spiked as Doc froze up like a prey animal being stared down by a predator. He fought his fight-or-flight response as he watched the plan begin to fall apart. The guard on the left noticed Doc's unusual behavior and began to walk over. The movement of the second guard seemed to snap Doc out of his paralysis and he began to fumble clumsily in his pockets, trying to reach his weapon. Both guards instantly reacted, the one who had originally approached Doc reaching out to grab him as the other began to bring his weapon to bear.

With the element of surprise gone, Jason reacted immediately; with an effort born out of fear, he put all his strength into pushing the hover cart and its massive load forward. It slammed into the second guard, who yelled out in surprise as he was driven into the wall. As soon as Jason felt the guard crushed between the cart and the wall, he killed power to the unit and it fell to the floor with a heavy thud that echoed up the passageway. With one threat temporarily neutralized, Jason looked over and saw Doc wrestling with the other guard for control of the large weapon he carried, and losing badly. The much stronger alien spun, with Doc still trying to hold on, and flung him into the wall. Doc had no sooner collapsed in a heap than the guard turned back towards the group, took aim, and fired. The shot resulted in a muffled yelp as someone behind Jason took a hit.

Jason didn't look to see who it was as he drew his own weapon and took aim at the first guard. With no hesitation he fired. The energy bolt lanced out and exploded against the chest plate of the guard's armor. The hit staggered him but didn't put him down, and after taking a step backward, he turned to engage Jason. After his first shot, Jason had immediately lowered into a crouch and raised his aim slightly. He only had one shot left. Whoever squeezed off first would win the fight. They fired simultaneously, the guard's hurried shot hitting the pod closest to Jason, showering the side of his face with hot sparks and bits of slag. Jason's shot, however, took the guard full in the face where he wore no armor. The result was dramatic as the headless body went rigid and collapsed to the floor.

Suddenly, more shots began to impact the walls around them; the pinned guard had freed his left arm and was now firing wildly into the passageway, unable to see where he was aiming. Ducking down, Jason waved to Twingo, "Weapon!" The engineer tossed Jason his own hold-out gun without hesitation. Catching it in stride, Jason hurried around the other side of the cart, opposite the guard's gun arm, and ended the engagement with a single shot.

After the short exchange of fire, everyone stood around, utterly stunned. Jason had to get them moving again. "You!" he said, pointing to Kage, "Get to work. Twingo, get Doc up and moving. Pilot, help me get these pods opened up." When nobody moved, Jason raised his voice, "NOW! The clock is ticking, people." This got them all moving as they went about their assigned tasks. He walked over and saw that one of their pilots hadn't made it, a smoking, charred hole in his uniform, center mass, where the guard had squeezed off a single shot. Jason didn't dwell on the loss of the individual past what it meant for the success of the mission; they were now short one pilot of the two required. They had been beyond lucky with the personnel that had been in the hold of the DL7 when they hatched this plan. He wasn't sure where this left them.

He moved over to the surviving pilot and began helping him unload Bondrass' thugs, laying them out on the deck. They were all still knocked out, luckily, although one had apparently lost control of his bladder while in the stasis pod. After they were all unpacked, Jason turned to his helper. "Okay, now move up this passageway about twenty meters and keep lookout. Haul ass back here and warn me if anyone comes down." The pilot nodded and shuffled up to the first turn of the dimly lit corridor. Jason went to pick up the first guard's weapon and then went back to the unconscious security personnel. He took a deep breath; this was the part he had been least looking forward to. He was a soldier, and he accepted that he may be called upon to kill in battle, but this was more of an execution. Methodically be began shooting energy bolts into the aliens, trying to place the shots in randomized locations. Ignoring the smell, he turned back to the others to see what progress was being made.

"Where are we at, Kage?" Jason asked the odd, four-armed being who was at the vault door control panel.

"Almost there. The computer accepted the guard's key card. Now I'm just trying to bypass the confirmation code." Jason noticed that the two smaller arms of the alien were pressed against the edges of the panel and what looked like streams of liquid metal were snaking out of his palms and breaking into tendrils that went through the gaps of the device. While fascinated, Jason was far too busy, and stressed, to ask about what he was doing. He walked over to where Twingo was helping Doc to his feet. He still looked shaky as he looked around at the carnage of the short, yet fierce firefight.

"It's not what you expected, is it?" Jason asked him gently.

"I'm sorry, Jason. I really thought I would be able to do it. I just ..." He paused when Jason raised his hand.

"It's fine, Doc. We're still in the game right now, but we've gotta move quickly. Every second we're out here exposed, our chances of getting caught increase exponentially." As if on cue, Kage let out a triumphant little whoop as the blast doors groaned slowly open. Jason, Twingo, and Doc raced over to him, Twingo grabbed the second guard's weapon as he got to the door. Jason whistled softly to get the pilot's attention and waved for him to come back to them. Once they had assembled, they set off into the chamber and cycled into the aft cargo airlock.

"This storage facility is actually a large, slip-capable cargo ship. It's backed up to this passageway and can exit through a secret tunnel. If The Vault is ever compromised, they'll simply close the doors and fly out of here with all the bosses' precious cargo intact," Doc said as they entered an enormous room lined with stasis pods and storage containers as far as the eye could see. "Decades of control over the underworld in this section of the galaxy has made them complacent. They pay for an around-the-clock flight crew but skimp on security. Lucky thing for us." They jogged a little over what Jason would have guessed to be a quarter mile before coming to a set of lift doors that were clearly marked as leading to the bridge. Jason and Twingo piled in and Jason held a hand up to stop the others.

"We're going up first to clear the bridge. I'll send the lift back down when it's safe. We can't risk losing any more of you this close to the objective," he said as the doors slid shut. When the lift started to move, Jason turned to Twingo, "You up for this?"

"I won't freeze up on you like Doc, if that's what you're asking."

"It is," Jason said simply as the lift slowed to a stop and the doors opened. Twingo was apparently familiar with this ship design as well and led point with Jason covering their flanks and rear. The first target they encountered was a violet-skinned alien getting a drink from the galley. Jason raised his weapon and dropped him without hesitation. Twingo indicated with his hand that the bridge was just forward of their position. Jason held up three fingers and then began a silent countdown; once he lowered his last finger, both broke into a run and rushed onto the bridge.

The two aliens on the bridge were the same species as Bondrass, and looked utterly shocked by their sudden appearance. Twingo shot the captain, who had been lounging in the command chair, as Jason took out the second crewman a split second later when he turned from a computer terminal along the back wall.

"Clear," Jason said out of habit. "Go back and get the others." As the engineer rushed back off the bridge, Jason scanned all the instruments to ensure they hadn't tripped an alarm with the weapon fire. From what he could tell, and what his implants were telling him, they were still operating under the radar. He honestly couldn't believe how lucky they'd been so far.

It was a couple of minutes later when he heard the rest of his team running onto the bridge. Kage went directly to the command console and began inputting commands at blinding speed with all four of his nimble hands. The pilot also wasted no time sitting at the helm and beginning his pre-flight sequences. "We're in luck," he said. "They were prepped for a fast launch. We're only a couple seconds from being flight capable."

"Same here," Kage said. "By the time you get off the ship, I'll be able to release the docking clamps from here. When you're ready, just pull the guard's key card from the slot and the blast doors will close. I can read that from here and will take that as a signal to launch."

"Are you two going to be able to handle this ship?" Jason asked, concerned about their plan with the loss of one of their pilots.

"No problem," Kage said confidently. "I can handle the other half of flight ops, but it might be helpful if Twingo stayed behind to monitor the main systems."

"Very good. Twingo, you're staying here. Doc, you're with me. Good luck, everyone. I'll see you guys at the rally point as soon as we can get there. We'll give you as much of a distraction as we can," Jason said brusquely before turning and walking off the bridge with Doc in tow. It took another five minutes to transit back to the entry of the storage ship and, mercifully, things were just as they had left them. Jason and Doc wasted no time getting the hover carts stowed in the ship, not bothering to secure the now-empty stasis pods. They then went about the gruesome job of arranging the bodies of the guards and Bondrass' men into what Jason hoped look like the aftermath of a savage firefight. He placed his own expended hold-out weapon in the hand of one of the security thugs he recognized from the flight to The Vault from Pinnacle Station and put Twingo's near the hand of another. He then returned the headless guard's weapon to its rightful owner before looking over at Doc. "Seem believable?"

"Seems like it," Doc said, looking around.

"Get ready to run then," Jason said as he reached up and yanked the key card out of the slot. The doors immediately began to close, much quicker than they had opened. Jason tossed the card through the opening before the doors closed completely and began to jog up the corridor towards the security archway. The pair hadn't made it very far when red strobes started flashing and an alarm started blaring. They felt a heavy jolt through the floor and felt the air pressure change slightly; the cargo ship had just blasted away from The Vault. Jason looked over to Doc in alarm and broke into a full sprint.

They broke out of the corridor and ran directly into pure chaos. The alarms had triggered a stampede out of the packed promenade as aliens tried to trample each other through the main security entrance to get to the secured hangar bay. They weren't aware of what the alarms were for, but they also didn't want to wait around to find out. Security personnel at the main entrance opened fire on the crowd but were quickly overwhelmed. The hangar entrance was also overrun as they tried to stem the tide, something Jason intended to take full advantage of. He and Doc ran full bore into the throng of aliens trying to escape and surged through the archway and into the open bay.

The mass of aliens that flooded into the secure hangar now had to contend with the security systems of the ships that were parked there as well. Powerful bolts of energy lanced out from the ships' guns causing massive casualties where they hit, seemingly indiscriminate. The air tingled with static electricity and the smell of ozone overpowered the odor of the alien throng. Just when he thought they were free and clear, Jason heard someone shout, "YOU! STOP!" Jason turned in time to see the guard Doc had talked to earlier taking aim at them with an ugly-looking weapon. He turned and bore down on the DL7 as fast as his legs would carry him. Doc, running directly in front of him, was keeping pace. Although waiting for it, he was still somewhat unprepared when it felt like someone hit him in the back with a sledgehammer, sending him sailing through the air and landing face down on the hangar deck.

Jason's vision was blurred and the pain in his jaw was excruciating where he had impacted the hangar floor. He tried to clear his head but couldn't focus or get his legs up under him as he began to be trampled by the panicked mob. He saw Doc run up the ramp of the gunship and realized he wasn't going to make it off the asteroid along with everyone else. He rolled over to face the guard, prepared to give an accounting of himself, but as he sat up he saw the guard, and the two behind him, dropped in their tracks by three well-placed plasma bolts. He was abruptly lifted off the floor like a sack of flour and vaguely aware that he was being carried across the floor towards his ship at a fast run. From the way he seemed to be floating over the rest of the crowd, he knew it had to be Crusher; he had taken out the guards and now he was carrying him back to the ship.

By the time Crusher reached the cargo bay, Jason's head had started to clear enough that he could somewhat function. When he was put back on the ground, he hit the controls to seal up the cargo bay and raise the ramp before shakily heading for the bridge as quickly as he could manage. He could hear Crusher's heavy footfalls right behind him as he raced through the ship. "Pilot! Turn the ship around! Put our nose to the blast doors," Jason yelled as he jumped into his customary copilot seat. The pilot grunted and twisted the controls, rotating the ship around on its landing gear so they were facing the heavy, and still closed, hangar doors. This was the last wrinkle in the plan Jason simply hadn't been able to plan for; he had no idea how they were going to get the gunship out of The Vault. He supposed they all could have left in the cargo ship, but the thought of leaving the DL7 behind was unconscionable to him.

"Looks like some people are getting impatient," the pilot said, pointing to a ship starting to lift off the floor on thrusters. The downwash from the ship sent aliens near that parking spot flying across the deck. Jason turned to say something to the pilot and noticed that his face was busted up pretty bad and he was leaning in the seat oddly. Before he could ask him what the hell happened, Crusher spoke.

"Commander, perhaps it would be prudent to arm the ship's weaponry. If we get an opportunity to run, we should be ready for anything," the enormous alien rumbled quietly. Jason answered him without taking his eyes off the pilot's injuries.

"Not a bad idea." He had a pretty good idea of what, or who, had happened to the pilot, and he was glad he had listened to his instincts. From his station he went about bringing the weapons online. He could feel the reactor start to automatically build power as the demand increased. While he was monitoring the offensive systems the pilot spoke up again.

"Oh, no!"

Jason snapped his head up again and watched the ship that had tried to launch earlier hover unsteadily past them, moving towards the exit. It swung about to face the hangar doors and let loose with two heavy particle beams. Since the station designers had never thought anyone would be trying to blast their way *out* of the hangar, the energy shields were only on the outside of the doors. Both beams impacted the metal with dramatic effect and began tracing a path around the perimeter of the portal, but the amount of slag and debris that was being blown back into the hangar threatened to damage the ship before it could cut its way through. Jason was thankful another small freighter was between the gunship and the doors as he could hear the smaller pieces pinging off their hull.

After five more seconds of continuous fire, which felt like five hours, the doors let go with a tortured shriek of distressed metal and blew out against the landing apron on the other side. The explosion from inside took out the energy shields, but the electrostatic barrier was miraculously still functioning and kept the atmosphere in. The aliens that weren't killed already during the escape attempt were now sprinting towards other ships, begging to be let aboard, or back through the archway out of the hangar.

"Get us out of here!" Jason snapped. He felt the ship bounce and rock, but they weren't moving.

"We're stuck! They've activated mag-locks on the deck and raised an interdiction field. The grav-drive is useless!" The pilot looked to be near panic. Truthfully, Jason wasn't far behind. Something Deetz had said a while ago kept bouncing around in his head though, something about the gravity drive.

"Bring the mains online! Thrust us off this pad and fire the repulsors to get us off of this rock!" Jason was relying heavily on his implants to help him if he needed to actually fire the ship's weapons. Thankfully, his connection to the ship's computer had been reestablished. He began to feel a low-frequency rumble that was steadily building in pitch and volume until he felt the ship start to shake and hunker down onto its nose-landing gear.

"Main engines at fifteen percent power, we're starting to move," the pilot said much more calmly. The ship bucked and strained against the magnetic locks, trying to hold the landing gear in place. Ever so slowly, the DL7 began to creep forward, its main engines howling within the confines of the hangar and violently buffeting the other ships nearby. The mag-locks finally lost their grip with a last little jerk and the ship rolled freely, and quite quickly, onto the main taxiway. The pilot yanked the power back to idle and was barely able to steer them to starboard to point them out towards space. The ship smoothly lifted off the deck as the ventral repulsors fired and the main engines nudged them through the shield and into the tunnel that led towards freedom. The pilot cycled the landing gear up and focused on flying them out.

Wisely, he resisted the urge to throttle up too much and risk bouncing down the tunnel walls. As it was, they still had a nasty surprise waiting for them when they emerged. At the last instant before the ship broke into open space, a missile strike hit the mouth of the tunnel and kicked up some heavy debris from around the edge. Most of this struck the gunship hard on the nose and the starboard side leading edge causing the ship to yaw sharply towards the tunnel wall. The ship bucked and a slew of alarms began scrolling down Jason's displays. "Shields!" Crusher shouted. Jason hunted around for, but couldn't find, the controls for the anti-collision or the combat shields. He gave up quickly.

"Computer, engage all external shielding," he said aloud. He got a confirmation through his implants that the shields had been engaged, but there were gaps in the coverage due to the damage to the starboard emitters from the debris impacts. "Be aware we have limited coverage on our starboard side. That slip-space emitter is only covered by the anti-collision shield right now."

"Got it," the pilot said as he commanded the engines to full power. The instant the ship emerged from the access tunnel, they were set upon by four small attack craft, all firing their plasma cannons. They weren't a huge threat, but with four of them engaging at once they had a better chance of landing a shot on the gunship's damaged side. Jason scanned the area with the sensors and could find no trace of the cargo ship. He hoped that was a good sign.

"Computer," Jason called out again, giving up completely on trying to decipher the manual controls, "activate point defense systems. Engage all targets currently firing on us."

"Acknowledged." The words had no sooner been uttered over the bridge PA when the big gunship opened up with its formidable arsenal. Plasma bolts shot out from turrets that had deployed all around the ship at Jason's command. Two of the small attack craft were destroyed instantly and a third was completely vaporized as it made the fatal mistake of crossing in front of the fleeing DL7; the main guns on the leading edges of the wings spat two brilliant red streaks into space and turned it into a cloud of ionized particles. They were quickly outrunning the last attacker. It wouldn't be able to get turned around and back into range before they made their first jump.

"Engaging slip-drive now," the pilot said smugly a moment before the ship winked out of existence in the space outside The Vault. Once they were safely in slip-space, Crusher walked calmly over to the pilot, grabbed a handful of his coveralls, and picked him up out of the chair with one hand, holding him out at arm's length. The pilot struggled mightily until Crusher flung him across the bridge with an overhand throw that would have carried the smaller being a good twenty meters had he not impacted the canopy first. Jason stood and stared in shock at the crumpled pilot and the bloody smudge on the canopy.

"Care to explain?" Jason asked, hoping this wasn't a precursor to Crusher killing them all with his bare hands and absconding with the ship.

"That vermin tried to steal the ship as soon as you were out sight," Crusher said calmly. "He first tried to enlist those of us you left behind, and when that failed he tried to seal himself on the bridge. I stopped him and told him I would deal with him after our escape, and so I did. Your instincts were very good, Commander." Crusher's quiet, dignified demeanor after such an act of pure violence unnerved Jason.

"Yeah ... thanks. But we still sorta needed him. I don't really know how to fly this thing," Jason said as he looked at the pilot's crumpled form. If he was still alive, he sure as hell wasn't going to be doing any flying anytime soon.

"Hmm," was all Crusher said, also looking at the pilot. "That is a problem." Doc appeared a moment later and walked towards Jason, pausing when he saw the carnage at the front of the bridge.

"So ... what'd I miss?"

"We're short one traitorous pilot. Oh ... and our only way to land the ship without killing us all," Jason said, shooting Crusher a glaring look. Enough to show his displeasure, but not enough to elicit a challenge. He hoped.

"Hmm, that's a problem," Doc said.

"So I've heard," Jason replied. "Any suggestions?" Doc didn't answer immediately. Instead, he walked over and checked the vitals of the pilot.

"He's still alive, barely. Let's get him to the infirmary and try to stabilize him. You come too, Jason. I may have an answer to our pilot shortage." Doc walked off the bridge, assuming one of them would bring the diminutive pilot. Jason looked pointedly at Crusher.

"It's your mess," he said. The big alien sighed and walked over to retrieve his handiwork. He was surprisingly gentle as he straightened the pilot out and cradled him in his arms to carry him down to the infirmary. Jason verified their countdown timer until they entered real-space was active and then followed.

Once the pilot was strapped down to the table, the automated medical systems began to work on him immediately, mostly pumping him full of medical nanites. Doc turned to Jason, "There's a way to impart the knowledge needed to fly the ship directly into your brain via the neural implant, but it's not customarily done so soon after the initial install."

"Why not?"

"It takes the neural implant time to learn your synaptic pathways. Implanting skills into your brain is quite intricate. This may be met with varying degrees of success."

"How varying?" Jason asked, almost certain he didn't want to know the answer.

"It could range from complete success to massive and permanent brain damage, although it'll likely hit somewhere in the high-middle range. Your brain has shown itself to be readily adaptable to the technology." Doc was looking at him intently.

"Screw it. Let's do it. Where do you need me?"

"Really?" Doc and Crusher asked in unison.

"Yes. If I think about it too long I won't do it, and we don't have much of a choice at this point."

"We could bring else someone out of stasis, or see if one of the others we released already has the necessary implants ..."

"No! Thanks, Doc, but no. This is my mission, I'm in command, and I'll accept the risks to see it completed," Jason said. He could see Crusher puff up his chest and nod with approval. *What the hell is he so impressed with? He's the reason we're in this mess.* Still half-afraid of the monster, Jason kept his thoughts to himself.

"Okay," Doc said quietly. "Let's do this in your quarters. You may as well be comfortable during this." He grabbed a long interface cable out of the case Jason's implants had originally been delivered in and gestured for him to lead the way.

Once in his room, Doc had Jason lay down on the bed on his back. He plugged one end of the cable he'd brought into a socket near the room's computer terminal and walked towards Jason with the other end. The cable flattened out on that end into what looked like a circular paddle about one inch in diameter. Doc reached under Jason's neck and placed the pad just above his collar. He could feel it adhere to his skin instantly. Doc then removed a memory chip from the case and began installing a software package on the ship's main computer via the terminal at Jason's desk. The software would allow the computer to connect to his neural implant through the interface cable.

"Now," Doc began, "I want you to visualize connecting to the interface I just put on your neck. Try to imagine your brain actually reaching out to touch it, almost as if your brain could move." Jason looked at him as if he was mad, but he did as he was asked. As soon as he began to visualize the absurd request, he was shocked to feel something crawling through his skin and then a sudden coolness, like the pad had been coated in a pain-relief gel.

"Excellent!" Doc was monitoring him through the terminal display on his desk. "You're a natural. In order for this high-level data transfer to work, there has to be a hard connection. It's also a safety measure that protects you in case someone is trying to establish a remote link to your brain. That visualization let your neural implant know you wished to establish a link and it sent nanite threads to the surface of your skin to complete the hard circuit with the interface. Keep that feeling in mind, it'll be useful in the future. Now, you're going to have to do this next part. I don't have the proper permissions to instruct the computer to begin an upload."

"What do I do?" Jason asked, more than a little apprehensive with what he was about to attempt.

"Tell the computer you want the full flight instruction set for the DL7 uploaded through your implant," Doc said.

"Computer, upload the full flight instruction set for the DL7 through my neural implant," Jason said aloud.

"Acknowledged. Establishing connection ..." Jason felt the patch on his neck go from cool to hot. "Connection established, do you wish to remain conscious during the upload?" Doc was frantically shaking his head no and waving his arms.

"No!"

"Acknowledged. Stand by for upload ..." Jason didn't hear another word as the computer commanded his neural input to put him to sleep.

Chapter 15

Damn this is getting old. Jason blinked his eyes as he slowly woke up from the data transfer in his dark room. He was beginning to lose count of how many times he'd either been put under or just plain been knocked out since this adventure began. He didn't feel anything on his neck so he reached behind him and found that the interface cable had disconnected from his skin on its own. He concentrated on how to fly the ship, but drew a blank. He wasn't sure how it was supposed to feel, but as far as he could tell, nothing was different except the feeling that he'd been laying on his back for too long. Rubbing his temples, he sat up in his bed.

"How do you feel, Commander?"

"SHIT!" Jason shouted as he jumped so high he actually fell halfway off the bed and became stuck between the exterior bulkhead and the bed. The lights came up and he could make out Crusher sitting in a chair by the door watching him curiously. His heart still pounding from the fright, he tried to salvage a bit of his dignity. "I'm doing okay. How are you?"

"I am well."

"That's good," Jason said as he tried to dislodge himself. After a moment of struggling, which must have looked absurd, he turned back to Crusher. "A little help?" With what looked suspiciously like a smile on his mouth, Crusher walked around the bed, grabbed Jason's arm, and effortlessly lifted him off the floor and set him on his feet. Straightening his clothes out, Jason walked out of the room without a word, leaving a quietly chuckling Crusher in his wake.

Jason headed to the infirmary to talk to Doc and was slightly surprised when Crusher kept walking and headed towards the cargo bay instead. Shrugging, he continued on and greeted Doc as he walked in. Doc threw him a preoccupied wave as he hovered over the pilot that Crusher had thrown into the canopy. As far as Jason could tell, he was still completely out. Doc tweaked one last thing on the tablet computer he was holding and looked up. "So ... do you feel okay?"

"Other than that monster Crusher scaring the shit out of me when I woke up, I'm just peachy," Jason said as he flopped down in one of the chairs.

"Yeah," Doc chuckled, "he stayed in the room guarding you the entire time you were out."

"Why?" Jason asked, both surprised and mildly creeped out.

"It's in his nature. You're his commander right now and his kind are fiercely loyal. Not only that, you freed him from a life of certain torment and probably a violent death."

"That's ... strange ... but I mean why guard me at all? It's not like this was even remotely close to the most dangerous thing I've faced since this all started," Jason said.

"Oh, that's right ... you were already out when we released the others. Crusher and I figured that having all the prisoners out of the stasis pods and mobile was in our best interests," Doc said, sitting across from Jason. "We may have to make a hasty exit at the rendezvous point. We were also tempting fate by keeping the units running on their own internal power for so long, but thankfully we didn't lose anyone. We've set them all up in the cargo bay and restricted their access to the rest of the ship. They're a mostly grateful bunch, but there are still more than a few dangerous individuals out there."

"Good thinking, I guess. How's he?" Jason gestured with his chin towards the pilot.

"Stable. He'll recover, surprisingly. You may want to talk to Crusher and impose some controls. If he's left to his own devices, someone could end up seriously hurt or killed," Doc said. Jason looked at him incredulously.

"I'm not telling that behemoth anything he can or can't do. My self-preservation instinct is too strong for that," he said.

"Your self-preservation instinct is questionable, at best—"

"Hey!"

"—and at any rate, he'll listen to you. Just tell him no killing or maiming until he asks first." Jason rolled his eyes at that and got up to leave.

"I need to get something to eat," he said as he walked out of the infirmary, intent on hitting up the galley before going to the bridge.

After a quick meal, he walked up to an empty bridge and stopped himself before he sat in the copilot seat. Instead, he walked back around and hopped into the pilot's seat and waited as it adjusted itself to his body. As soon as he laid eyes on the controls at the helm, it was like someone opened the floodgates in his brain. He instinctively knew what every control did and what each display represented without having to consciously think about it. He also now understood how the gravity drive and main engines complemented each other and when each was appropriate; he even knew at what speed the lifting body would stall within an atmosphere and when the repulsors would kick in. It went beyond simple memorization: he truly knew what he needed to do in order to fly the DL7. *I'd have killed for this implant back in high school.* He observed that they were on the final leg to their destination with forty-two hours remaining until they meshed into real-space. That would mean he had been out for around thirty-six hours.

"Commander Burke, please come to the cargo bay," Doc's voice floated through the ship's PA. Jason's nerves were already frayed as it was; he fervently hoped there was no new disaster waiting for him in the cargo bay.

"On my way," he said as he hopped out of his chair and headed aft. Entering the cargo bay, he paused. There were twenty-two aliens milling around on the deck with all but one stasis pod pushed up against the port side of the bay. Mats were scattered throughout the cargo bay where the freed prisoners had obviously been sleeping. Jason spotted Doc and Crusher standing by the last stasis pod that still had power applied. Crusher was still armed with the plasma carbine and eyeing the prisoners with thinly veiled menace. Jason sighed, realizing he would indeed have to have a talk with him.

"What's this?"

"The last prisoner," Doc said. "But we're a little unsure how to handle him." Jason peered into the pod and let out an audible gasp at what he saw. Nestled in the pod was a synth, but nothing like Deetz. This machine was easily two meters tall and looked heavily armored. Even his face was armored with only the eyes visible.

"Holy shit!"

"Indeed. He's a battlesynth, a rarity even among such a rare species," Doc said, eyeing the bulky synth. "The issue is that he's loaded with integrated weaponry and he's unbelievable strong. If we let him loose in here and he becomes disagreeable, the entire ship is at risk."

"I see your point. Is there any way to only activate his cognitive functions so we can talk to him?" Jason asked. Doc turned and began poking at the controls of the stasis pod before answering.

"It appears we can. You want to wake him?" he asked.

"Yeah, let's talk to him and see what's what. Keep your hand on the control to shut him down again if it goes wrong," Jason said. After a few more seconds, the head of the synth snapped up and the eyes moved, focusing first on Jason and then sweeping the room.

"Identify yourself," the synth demanded.

"I'm Commander Jason Burke. My associates are Dr. Ma'Fredich and Crusher," Jason said.

"I recognize you," the synth said to Crusher. "Am I to understand we've been delivered to our new keepers?" The tone was unmistakably contemptuous.

"You understand wrong," Crusher said. "These men have gone to great risk to rescue us."

"Rescue?" the synth said skeptically. "To what end?"

"To whatever end we choose. We're to be freed." Crusher's tone was surprisingly gentle as he addressed the synth.

"What's your name?" Jason asked, trying to maintain control of the conversation.

"I am Combat Unit 777," the synth said.

"You've got to be kidding me … Your name is a serial number?" Jason asked, the cliché of it almost too much for him. "You don't have a name besides that?"

"Why would I?" 777 seemed genuinely confused. "I do not interact with biologicals on a social level and my designation is sufficient to accomplish my tasking."

"Fair enough," Jason said. "So, Lucky 777, if we restore the rest of your functions and let you out, do you promise not to destroy the ship, or us, until we land and you can go your own way?" The synth looked at Jason and then to Crusher, who nodded to him.

"I am no threat to you or your vessel. I do wish to be left alone, however," 777 said quietly.

"No problem. Doc, go ahead and fire him up and release the restraints." Jason knew he was taking a huge risk, but the idea of keeping 777 chained up was repugnant to him. Freedom for some but not for all? That wasn't what he had risked his life for at The Vault, so he'd take his chances and hope his decision didn't end in a lunatic synth butchering everyone in the cargo bay. Looking at the impressive machine, Jason had his doubts that even Crusher would fare too well against him.

777's whole body twitched once as Doc restored full system control to him. After he was clearly supporting his own weight on his legs, they popped the restraints off and let him step out of the pod. "Do I need to stay in here with them?" he asked distrustfully, almost fearfully as he looked at the huddle of other prisoners. Jason thought hard about that one. Letting him out of the pod was one thing, but letting him into the guts of the ship was quite another.

"Where would you be most comfortable?" Jason asked, hoping to reach a compromise.

"I would prefer to remain with you three," he said, indicating Jason, Doc, and Crusher. Jason looked to Doc, who shrugged noncommittally.

"Follow us then," Jason said to 777. "Everyone else," he addressed the others who were leerily watching the synth move about and exercise his servos, "we're nearly to our destination. Once we land we'll meet up with the others we've freed and discuss what the next move is. I'm guessing for a lot of you it'll be a trip home." The other three followed Jason out of the cargo bay to the sound of cheers and clapping. They made their way to the bridge where Jason immediately slouched back into the pilot's seat as 777 slowly walked around the bridge following Crusher and Doc.

"How much longer?" Doc asked.

"About another thirty-two hours," Jason said after a glance at his displays. "I'll take first watch if you guys want to grab some sleep. You can relieve me and then I'll take a quick power nap before we come out of slip-space." Doc and Crusher grudgingly agreed and left him alone on the bridge with 777.

Jason was content to let the synth stand off to the side in silence as he continued to familiarize himself with the ship's controls to reinforce his newly acquired skills. 777 was the first to speak. "Commander, why did you call me Lucky 777?"

"Hmm? Oh … on my world the number seven is considered lucky. Since you're triple-seven, I would have to say that you're three times lucky." Jason regretted his glib response after he said it. The synth had just recently been a packaged piece of property, after all. He could hardly consider him "lucky," all things considered.

"Lucky. I suppose I would have to consider myself lucky if I thought about it," 777 said quietly. "I was abducted to serve a cruel purpose, of that I am sure. Most consider my kind to be simply highly advanced machines: intelligent, but ultimately just a piece of equipment. Once they realize we cannot be reprogrammed or coerced, they usually dispose of us."

"So your design doesn't allow you to be controlled by reprogramming?"

"No. Our personalities and processing structure are unique to each individual. This was done intentionally. We were given free will by our creators and it cannot be taken away." 777's choice of words struck home for Jason as he thought about the Declaration of Independence from his own country. In many ways it seemed the synths would never be free, rather unwelcome and unrecognized as free-thinking beings by the majority of governments. He was saddened to think he had freed this sentient being only to release him into an uncaring galaxy to make his own way.

The pair fell silent for a while as each was lost in his own thoughts. Jason got up to go get a mug of chroot when 777's hand reached out to touch his shoulder.

"Commander, thank you for freeing me." Jason put his own hand on the synth's shoulder in turn.

"You're welcome," he said simply, unable to think of anything else to say that wouldn't sound trite.

Jason milled about in the galley for a little while, thinking about the very real consequences of his recent actions. He had, without a doubt, just formed some powerful enemies. He didn't know exactly how powerful these crime lords might be, but he was certain they were at least strong enough to cause serious problems for Earth if they ever found out where he had come from. He wracked his brain to think of a way to keep his home planet a secret, but by virtue of having to take a ship back to Earth at least once to get home he always ran the risk of at least one other knowing its location.

He continued to mull things over in his head until he heard footsteps approaching from the direction of crew berthing. Looking up, he saw Crusher walking towards him while in the middle of an open-mouthed, feline-like yawn. "Where is 777?"

"Up on the bridge. We talked a bit and I don't think there's any risk in letting him stay up there alone," Jason said sleepily, the long day catching up with him.

"Nor do I," Crusher said. "Go ahead and get some sleep, Commander. I'd prefer you to be well rested before attempting your first landfall."

"That may not make a huge difference," Jason mumbled as he walked by on the way to his quarters.

Chapter 16

Sitting in the pilot's seat, Jason felt a growing sense of dread as the counter ticked off the final few minutes before the ship would drop back into real-space. He felt well-rested and he had his friends around him, but none of them had ever made a landing either so for now they were more or less useless. Crusher had claimed the copilot's seat and Doc was sitting at one of the sensor stations. 777 seemed to have an aversion to sitting, so he stood behind Jason's seat so he could see both the displays and the view outside.

The brief flash and lurch Jason now associated with slip transitions marked their arrival into the destination system. He gave the instruments a glance while the canopy returned to translucent before engaging the grav-drive and angling them onto a course to intercept the fourth planet: a massive, rocky "super-Earth" that had a habitable but deserted moon orbiting it. The planet itself also harbored life, but the massive gravity would be deadly to all of them.

Easing the ship into a low orbit, Jason asked the computer to begin scanning the surface and, sure enough, they spotted the cargo ship his friends had taken from The Vault. Still using the grav-drive, he slowed the ship further and dipped the nose down to begin entering the atmosphere. He could opt to use a tremendous amount of power and simply stop the ship and descend straight to their landing target, but any ship in the system would see them on their sensors if they were looking for any gravitational anomalies.

Once they had burned through the upper atmosphere, Jason took manual control of the ship and started flying them towards the beacon on his display that indicated where the cargo ship was. Flying the DL7 wasn't as difficult as he had imagined, but it certainly wasn't something he would have been able to figure out on his own.

He overflew the cargo ship and saw a few dozen aliens standing in the tall grass, waving enthusiastically at them. He pulled the gunship into a tight circle and tried to bring it to a hover. He soon realized, however, that possessing the knowledge of how to fly the ship and having the muscle memory and instincts honed from countless hours of experience were two very different things. The nose dipped precariously, causing the drives to whine in protest as they fought to level the ship out. Then he overcorrected and brought the nose up too sharply and began to bleed off precious altitude as they slid backwards. Thankfully his companions kept quiet save for the occasional muttered curse or sharp intake of breath as Jason was finally able to get the ship back under control after some more unintended aerobatics and began a wobbly descent to the surface. He cycled the landing gear at one-hundred feet and let the computer take over as the DL7 touched down with a gentle bump.

"Well that wasn't so bad," Jason said to himself. Turning to his crewmates he asked, "Right?" Nobody answered as they walked off the bridge. He thought he heard Crusher mutter something about wishing he had been back in his stasis pod. "Everybody's a critic," Jason said as he secured the drives and leveled the ship on its landing gear. The last thing he did was release the security hold on the cargo ramp before departing the bridge.

He made his way back to the cargo bay by way of the armory, grabbing a plasma sidearm and his railgun. He didn't necessarily distrust the former prisoners outside, but he didn't exactly trust them either. He walked out and saw the ramp was already down and most of the passengers had already disembarked. A larger-than-life laugh coming from just outside let Jason know Twingo had arrived to greet them. Smiling, he broke into a jog to go meet up with his friend as he slung the railgun over his shoulder. Twingo and Doc were already trying to compare who had the harder time of escaping The Vault when he walked down the ramp. Kage and Crusher stood by as spectators, and 777 had moved somewhat apart from the others, appearing uncertain as to what he should be doing.

"Nice landing, Jason! We were all about to take cover back in the ship before you finally got this beast under control," Twingo called out with a laugh.

"Piss off," Jason laughed as he grabbed the engineer into a bear hug, lifting him off the ground. They all laughed good naturedly at Jason's expense and were generally in high spirits; they had pulled it off and the natural high from an accomplished mission was potent.

"You won't believe what's in that ship," Twingo was saying. "It wasn't just stasis pods: the bosses had cargo containers full of precious metals and other high-value items. We've released all the prisoners, staged all the cargo, and dumped the pods."

"So do they have a full flight crew for that ship?" Jason asked. When Twingo and Kage both nodded, Jason continued, "I figure once they get it unloaded they can board and head to whichever civilized planet they choose. Most of them were taken against their will and aren't criminals. Let's leave it to the authorities to start getting them back home. Otherwise, we'll be ferrying them back and forth for years."

"That's a good idea, but how do they explain how they obtained the ship and fled The Vault without getting us involved?" Doc asked.

"We still have the dead flight crew and some of Bondrass' men. They can spin it that a pod malfunctioned and they were able to release the others and overpower the crew, stealing the ship," Twingo offered.

"It's fairly weak," Jason said with a frown. "But it's the best we have. Get with the replacement flight crew and try to hash out the details and then tell everyone else they didn't know anything until they were brought out of stasis, which is more or less the truth."

"So what's next for us?" Twingo asked. Doc cut Jason off before he could even open his mouth fully to speak.

"There's still one more thing we should do before we call this done," Doc said quickly. "Bondrass wasn't just into abduction and trafficking. Part of what I did for him involved some pretty heavy, and illegal, genetic engineering. He has a vast, automated facility into which he's invested a substantial part of his fortune. Taking it out would break him."

"Doc," Jason spoke up first, "freeing the people in The Vault was a righteous move, and it was in parallel with our need to escape ourselves. But this seems to be nothing but revenge, which I understand. Bondrass deserves that, and much more, for what he did to you. But, you have to understand … we were incredibly lucky on this mission. There's no way that we should have been able to get away that easily."

"I know what I'm asking," Doc said, "and I know that some of you would like to walk away and go home now while we still can. I'm asking you to trust me in that the implications of letting this facility continue to exist are far more profound than any one crime boss' wallet. It's not likely I'll ever be in a position again to really do something about it either." He gestured to the hissing DL7 gunship as he finished. Once Doc stopped talking, Jason realized that they were all looking at him, waiting to see what his answer would be. He looked away from them for a moment and out over the alien landscape of the moon. The planet was rising up over the horizon to share the sky with the primary star and the effect was simply breathtaking.

After a moment's deliberation, Jason spoke again. "You're asking too much," he insisted. "We were more or less forced into action in this instance. You're talking about a deliberate assault on a civilian target. I may not be up on all the ins and outs of legalities in this part of the galaxy, but I have to believe that what you're proposing is highly criminal."

"Jason, you've personally killed nearly ten beings since I've met you. You didn't seem overly concerned about legal complications then …"

"That is NOT the way to get my cooperation!" Jason shouted, jabbing a finger into Doc's chest for emphasis, suddenly irate. "A situation born out of self-defense is entirely different than premeditated killing, and make no mistake: firing on a building from a ship is no different than shooting someone with a gun. As I remember it, your hesitation almost got *all* of us killed … Where was your moral high ground after I killed that guard to save your life?" The rest of the crew stood motionless, watching the increasingly hostile exchange between the two. Jason and Doc stared at each other for a few more tense seconds.

"You're right, Jason. I was out of line," Doc conceded, his shoulders slumping forward in defeat. "I'm sorry." Jason drew in a breath to deliver another blistering retort, still seething, and then stopped himself. He slowly let his breath escape between his lips, his anger ebbing away with it.

"It's fine, Doc. I understand … I really do," Jason said softly.

"Guys," Twingo interjected once a lot of the heat had bled off the conversation, "why don't we talk about this later, once we've had some time to process everything we've just been through. I can see your side, Jason, and I'm inclined to agree with you. Attacking random targets will likely get us tossed down into a deep, dark hole for a long time. But there's no harm in hearing him out."

"We've come this far together," Jason said to everyone, but looking Doc in the eye. "If you're telling me this is something that needs to be done, then I guess we need to at least discuss it. Either way, it seems we're stuck with each other for at least the foreseeable future. I'm assuming we're all leaving on this ship together, right, guys?"

"I'm in," Twingo added instantly. "Crusher?"

"I'm with Commander Burke for as long as he needs me."

"You guys have a spot for me?" Kage asked hopefully. "I don't really have anywhere else to go and I like how this outfit operates." Jason looked at the others and shrugged.

"Why not?" Jason said. Looking up, he spotted 777 walking back towards their group. "Hey, Lucky 7, what can I do for you?"

"I apologize in advance for eavesdropping, Commander," he started. "But I would like to join your crew as well. There is no place for me where the others are going, and I am certain I can be of use."

"Glad to have you," Jason said after seeing Crusher perk up at the notion of 777 joining their crew. He seemed to have a serious soft spot for the synth for whatever reason.

"What are we going to do with Deetz?" Twingo asked, changing the subject.

"Aw shit! I completely forgot about that asshole," Jason swore. "Come on, let's go deal with this now." He marched back up the ramp without waiting for a response.

Deetz was right where they'd left him, powered down and restrained in the heavy chair in Engineering. The six-person crew stood in a semi-circle around him.

"So, what are we going to do with him?" Doc asked, looking at Jason.

"Lucky, your kind is few and far between anymore, correct?" Jason asked.

"Yes, Commander. We are a species that is slowly going extinct. When the last of us goes offline, that will be the end of the synthetics," Lucky confirmed. Jason weighed his options. Destroying Deetz was certainly the safest, and most permanent, course of action. But the thought that he might be contributing to a species' extinction wasn't pleasant either. Staring at the still form in the chair, he knew what his decision had to be, so there was no point in dragging it out further than necessary.

"We're not going to kill him," Jason said. "Turn him on, Twingo." Without a word, the engineer entered some commands on a tablet computer he had grabbed off a work bench. Deetz twitched and raised his head as he came back online.

"Hello, Deetz. Nice nap?"

"Why have you done this, Jason?" Deetz asked.

"You've got to be kidding me, you fucking weasel. What was your deal with Bondrass to turn me over?" Jason was quickly losing both his patience and his temper. Deetz flinched at the mention of the crime boss.

"So, you found out. How clever of you."

"This is true then?" Lucky asked. "You were going to sell these men for personal gain?"

"What do you care?" Deetz sneered. "These are the same biologicals that would use you as a weapon with no concern for your safety or sanity, Combat Unit 777. You're nothing but an expendable resource."

"Not to me he isn't," Jason said forcefully, not interested in a protracted philosophical debate. "And despite being a slimy piece of trash, neither are you. As I understand it you're a fading species, and I won't contribute to that. Not today, at least. You're going to get on the ship that's sitting outside with all the other prisoners that we freed from The Vault and you're going to fly out of here, far, far away from me. This is a one-time reprieve. I catch you near me again and I'll shut you down. Understood?"

"Yes," Deetz said, defeated. Jason gestured for Twingo to release the clamps and allow Deetz to walk off the ship under his own power. He trudged out of Engineering, not even considering trying anything foolish with the powerful battlesynth right behind him. Once they reached the bottom of the ramp Jason simply pointed to the waiting ship across the field.

"Go," he said before turning his back on the synth.

It was nearly twelve hours of back-breaking work later when the crew of the gunship watched the enormous cargo hauler lumber into the sky on an artificial gravity well and thrusters, both of which played hell with Jason's equilibrium. They stood watching until it was just a speck in the sky before heading back up the ramp. The cargo bay was now flush with crates and pallets loaded with precious metals, exotic weaponry, and hard currency sponsored by governments that still honored non-traceable bills. The crew shuffled up to the lounge area wearily (except for Lucky, who never tired) and sunk into the sofas.

"So do we talk this out now? Or wait until tomorrow?" Doc asked.

"Fuck that. Anything we talk about now is likely to be meaningless. I'm wiped out so I'm going to bed," Jason said as he got up. "Computer, lock the ship up, ground defense protocol alpha."

"Acknowledged."

"I will stay on the bridge and monitor our defenses, Commander. I require no rest," Lucky offered, still standing while the others sat.

"Look at you, Lucky 7, earning your keep already," Jason said, patting the synth on the back as he walked by. "Thanks. Let me know if you need anything, I'll be in my quarters. Goodnight, all."

Jason went to his quarters, kicked his boots off after laying his weapons on the desk, and, for the first time in weeks, fell into a deep, untroubled sleep. The rest of the crew disbursed slowly and found their way to their bunks. On the bridge, Combat Unit 777 stood like a sentinel, every sensor alert. As the rest of the crew slept, the battlesynth stood watch and evaluated its existence and, for the first time since coming online, felt some small sense of belonging. He hoped it wasn't fleeting.

Chapter 17

The battlesynth descended from the bridge when he heard the crew stirring down in the galley. He approached the group and was waved over.

"Good morning, Lucky! Or whatever time it really is," Twingo called out to him.

"Good morning, Twingo. Commander. Crewmates," Lucky said respectfully as he moved to the end of the high-top table the crew was eating at. "I trust everyone slept well."

"Like a baby with you standing watch," Jason said between bites. "First good sleep I've had since this debacle started."

"We're going to discuss the possibility of our next operation after we eat," Doc said to the synth. "We'd appreciate if you'd lend us whatever insight you might have."

"It would be my pleasure," Lucky said.

Twenty minutes later they were all crammed into the small meeting room on the upper deck, aft and port from the bridge, discussing their plan of attack on the facility Doc swore was a critical target.

"Okay, Doc. Now that we're all rested, fed, and calm … try to convince us we need to hit this target," Jason said as he sat down in one of the chairs.

"Very well," Doc began, activating the main wall display. "This is the planet Kaldsh-4, a standard-sized, lightly industrialized planet with a small population. It's mostly just large tracts of agricultural land that support the food demands of the heavily populated core planets."

Jason settled back as Doc continued to lead the briefing since he had detailed intel on the target. In fact, he had incredibly precise locations and schematics for the facility thanks to a hidden, encrypted memory chip he had pulled out of the tablet computer he had brought on board with him at Pinnacle Station, so much so that it aroused Jason's suspicion about how involved he really was in Bondrass' operations.

After an hour of back and forth, the team decided that a direct approach would probably be best. The facility wasn't heavily fortified as it employed a "hiding in plain sight" approach to secrecy. It was also not heavily staffed, another plus since most of the crew wanted to avoid too much collateral damage and casual killing during the operation. The heavy arsenal the gunship carried made it possible for them to directly attack the target without too much risk. Doc was also adamant that they had to capture, or kill, a specific target he swore would be onsite. He actually insisted that this objective was more important that the destruction of the complex itself. Crusher and Lucky immediately volunteered for this job, but Doc said the target would not put up much of a fight; she was an academic, not a warrior.

"Her name is Dr. Jevara Da'Chelic. Here's a picture of her," Doc was saying as he worked the controls for the room's main display. The picture looked like a typical security badge mug shot and was of a female of the same species as the doctor. She had shoulder length, jet black hair (compared to Doc's bald head) and looked to be quite a bit younger as well.

"Why is she so dangerous, Doc?" Jason asked.

"She's really the linchpin to the whole operation. She's not necessarily the most brilliant scientist in the program, but she is the best at organizing the research across disciplines and keeping the project on track. Losing her will set them back years." Doc looked at the picture wistfully for just a split second. It wasn't much, but it didn't escape Jason's notice.

"And if this facility is left online, you're saying it poses a grave and immediate danger to a large number of people?"

"That's exactly what I'm saying. I can't overstate the risk in letting them continue this operation. There isn't a world that wouldn't be affected by what they're planning, including uninitiated planets like your own Earth," Doc fell silent and stood at the head of the table, waiting.

"Well … I'm not completely sold, but I'm not saying no either," Jason said carefully. "Let's go ahead and start planning for a tactical strike on the facility and we'll launch out shortly after. Once we're there, if it doesn't seem right, or even possible at all, I'm pulling the plug and we're bugging out."

"I can't ask for more than that, Commander. Thank you," Doc said with a slight nod.

Jason's real fear was that Doc wasn't overstating the case and Earth would indeed be at risk by whatever was being cooked up in the genetics lab. It didn't lessen the risk of what they were being asked to do, but at least it was something tangible he could grasp onto if he actually did go through with the unprovoked attack on a civilian target.

They adjourned the meeting and Jason dismissed them to individually prepare for their role in the upcoming festivities. He had his own preparations to make, but first he followed Doc back to the infirmary to have a word with him while he was away from the others. "I know we've beat this to death, but you're one-hundred percent certain this needs to be done? If it's such a risk, why not just alert the authorities?"

"Authorities," Doc snorted with disgust. "You think I haven't tried that? I left an anonymous tip that led to an exhaustive investigation of the place. They found nothing that led to a single arrest or indictment despite the very specific information I had provided. Bondrass suspected I had notified the ConFed Investigative Services and took it out on both me and my sister." He shuddered involuntarily as he recalled that particular horror.

"So what is this place, exactly? You have to give me something, Doc. You're asking us to risk a lot on faith. The others are all trusting you to be on the level about this," Jason said, trying a different tact.

"They're following you, Jason. Their decision has little to do with me. I wish I could answer your question in a way that would satisfy you, and I'm not being mysterious just for the sake of keeping secrets, but what you don't know you can't be forced to divulge if the law, or our enemies, ever catches up with us." Doc's answer left a cold lump in Jason's gut.

"Give me the broad strokes then," he said.

"It's a genetics research and production facility, the first of many planned. All I will say is that the work there could change the balance of power in this part of the galaxy in a profound way," Doc said as he leaned back against the medical bed. "Bondrass is a facilitator in this instance. He's the front for other interested parties that can't actively be associated with this sort of work as it's highly illegal."

"You're talking about a conspiracy, and that usually means government," Jason said.

"Very good, Commander. More than one, in this case. Or more accurately, interested parties within certain governments. That's as much as I feel I should tell you, Jason. Again, I'm asking for this leap of faith from you with the purest of intentions." While Jason was good at reading body language, his inexperience with Doc's species made it impossible for him to tell if he was being played.

"So what's their ultimate goal?" Jason asked.

"The usual," Doc shrugged. "Power and control. As happens from time to time, there are some that feel the great unwashed masses exist only to support the few elite, and once in a great while these people are in an actionable position to try and make it a reality."

"Well," Jason began slowly as he stood up, "my decision hasn't changed; I'm willing to put it on the line again if this is really that serious, but I'm not sure I'm willing to ask the others to do the same." He turned and walked towards the exit when Doc spoke up again.

"It is that serious, Jason. I wouldn't have asked otherwise." Jason simply nodded and walked back to the bridge. If they were going to be rushing headlong into another fight he had better get his shit together when it came to flying the ship.

Chapter 18

Much to Jason's relief, and delight, the ship had a simulation mode that allowed him to get some real seat-time at the helm. It literally turned the gunship's bridge into a full-motion simulator with a level of fidelity simulator engineers on Earth could only dream about. The grav-plating of the deck, the projection displays on the canopy, and all the controls and instruments were utilized by the computer to create an experience that was impossible to distinguish from actually flying. The beauty of it was that it allowed for all the bridge crew to participate in the same training scenario. His first instinct was to have Crusher fly in the copilot seat and operate the sensors and weapons, but the big warrior had almost no finesse and even less patience when it came to operating the ship's systems. He had also made it clear he had no interest in participating in the simulator training. With no genuine danger, he simply didn't see the point.

So with Crusher taking himself out of the running, Jason went a completely different direction and put Kage in the copilot seat. This ended up being a much better fit. The smaller alien was not only a natural at manipulating the controls, but his own set of unique neural implants allowed him to meld with the ship in a way that none of the others could. This solidified the crewing decisions Jason needed to make before they attempted their next mission; he, Kage and Doc would be on the bridge (unless there was a medical emergency), Twingo would be in Engineering, and Crusher and Lucky would be in full kit in the armory in case they needed boots on the ground.

Even with Jason's ability to have information pumped into his brain via the neural implant, the training wasn't all smooth sailing. He struggled to pilot the ship as the unfamiliar information he had injected in his head clashed with his instincts developed from what he knew about flying airplanes on Earth. Twingo had been on the bridge trying to help him over the rough patch, but even his patience was wearing thin. After a particularly miserable effort in which Jason had, yet again, crashed the ship, the short alien rubbed his head and squinted at the ceiling in frustration.

"Maybe if you understood more about how the ship actually flew it would help," he said.

"You think so?" Jason asked.

"It certainly couldn't hurt," Twingo muttered. "Okay, you keep trying to fly this as if it was an atmospheric aircraft with lift surfaces. You need to unlearn that. This ship moves by manipulating gravity. Let's start with the basics … What is gravity?"

"The force an object exerts on another in space," Jason said, feeling like a child being lectured.

"Incorrect. Gravity is the effect an object in space has on space itself. Think of space-time as a large bed sheet. Now drop a large ball in the middle, and a smaller ball near the edge, and what happens? The smaller ball rolls towards the larger, right? Why is that?" Twingo seemed to be struggling to find analogies the human could relate to.

"The smaller ball rolls down the impression on the sheet left by the larger one," Jason said.

"Exactly. It isn't because the smaller ball is attracted to the larger ball as if it were magnetic. Now, that's how the gravimetric engines of a starship work; they create localized gravity distortions that can be used to propel the ship. By changing the nature of the distortion we can change the speed and attitude of the ship at will; it's like the ship is gliding down a perpetual slope, but we continually change the pitch and direction of the slope."

"Then why have such large main engines as well?" Jason asked.

"Grav-drives are fantastic, but fickle. Their fields can be interrupted by gravimetric projectors, other drive fields, or natural occurrences in space. On something like that cargo hauler we stole, that isn't a huge deal. But on a ship like this, being left powerless isn't an option. So Jepsen also fitted her with some of the biggest thrusting motors *I've* ever seen." Twingo had moved over to lean against the console during his impromptu class. After having a bit more depth of knowledge in the ship's operations, the rest of Jason's training time seemed to be much more productive. He got to where he rarely killed them all during simulations and was starting to get the hang of transitioning the ship from void flying to flying in an atmosphere.

Their last day on the moon, Jason ran them through a specially developed training sim that was as close as he could make to what they would actually face based on Doc's information. They ran through it three times with no major hang-ups and a successful outcome each session. Jason was especially pleased, and somewhat surprised, at how well the crew was meshing. The personality differences seemed to complement each other rather than be a source of conflict, and each member went about his job without complaint. As they all sat in the galley that evening, Jason allowed himself a small sliver of hope that they would not only take out their target, but live to hoist a beer afterwards.

After the evening meal, Jason went outside to inspect the hull with Twingo to see where the damage control bots had repaired the impact damage they had sustained fleeing The Vault. As bad as it had initially looked, the damage proved to be mostly superficial and was easily erased by the small automated repair crew. After that, they performed a full checkout on the ship's power plant, engines, and weaponry; everything was full mission capable, so Jason saw no point in delaying.

They lifted off from the moon's surface as the primary star was just setting on the horizon. Jason flew them on a lazy arc out of orbit towards the edge of the system before engaging the slip-drive and sending them hurtling towards their objective. Once safely in slip-space, he left Lucky on the bridge for the nightly watch and went to bed with the rest of the crew; the next couple of days would likely be long and arduous.

Chapter 19

The gunship emerged into real-space just outside the heliopause of the Kaldsh system approximately fifty-two hours after they left the safety of the moon they'd been camped on. Jason waited for Kage to let him know if they'd damaged anything during the flight; he'd pushed the ship pretty hard to try and make up the time they'd lost sitting on the moon effecting repairs and training. "We're still FMC, Commander," Kage said evenly, "you're clear to begin maneuvering." FMC stood for Fully Mission Capable, and was an acronym from Jason's time in the USAF that he used out of habit that the rest of the crew had begun to pick up on and work into their own lexicon.

"Understood," Jason said. "Grav-drive coming online and turning on course for the fourth planet." They were following a commercial shipping lane in-system, so they weren't concerned about the gravity drive's signature being detected. Jason was keeping the reactor power down low enough that it wouldn't raise the suspicion of anyone who happened to be looking. "We're less than two hours out, team," he said over the ship's PA. "Everyone stay loose."

The gunship slid through the system unchallenged before achieving a high parking orbit that would be common for a cargo vessel that was waiting on clearance to make landfall. They made three complete orbits around the planet, a green, lush-looking world with lots of surface water, mapping the ground with their sensors on each pass. Kage easily deflected inquiries by the planet's ground controllers by claiming they were a courier ship that was repairing a flaky drive before attempting a landing.

Doc and Kage spotted the facility fairly quickly thanks to the intel they already had, otherwise it may have been impossible to find. It was a non-descript series of buildings that was on the outskirts of an industrial district outside one of the planet's smaller cities, but it also had employed a dampening field that hid its power signature from orbital sensors. Doc was able to penetrate the field by knowing the frequency and modulation of the ground emitters. The picture wasn't very clear, but it was enough for them to get target locks on specific areas of the compound.

"You still sure about everything down there, Doc?" Jason asked, standing over the doctor's shoulder and looking at the display. He was acutely aware he was about to launch an unprovoked attack on a civilian target, in a populated area, without any warning or formal declaration of intent.

"It's exactly as I left it. I would have assumed once I disappeared they would have begun shutting this place down, or at least started moving everything, but I don't see any unusual activity down there," he said, looking back at Jason. "We're clear to engage, Commander."

"Okay," Jason said, walking back to his seat. "Begin feeding target coordinates to Kage, Doc." He addressed the rest of the crew over the PA, "It's almost showtime, boys. Everyone switch coms over to open channel and get ready to commence operations."

"Engineering, checking in," said Twingo.

"Ground assault, ready to go," Crusher checked in for himself and Lucky.

Jason took a couple of slow breaths to steady himself and tried to tamp down the adrenaline spike he felt as the ship crossed the terminator and into daylight. "Ten seconds," he told his crew. He nodded to Kage who armed the ship's offensive and defensive systems. This was the point of no return. The power surge of their weapons coming online would easily be spotted by the ground control sensors. The lights on the bridge dimmed and red-light pipes glowed on the floor, illuminating the walkways.

"TacCon Delta," Kage reported, telling Jason that the gunship was now in tactical condition "Delta," meaning all weapons were powered and armed and shields were at full power. Jason could see on his com board that the planet's ground controllers were trying to hail them; he muted them and ignored the flashing alert. He tensed up and waited for the countdown on his center display to reach zero.

When the countdown timer disappeared, Jason shoved the nose hard over and dove towards the planet. He crossed through a transfer orbit, narrowly missing an oversized, underpowered cargo hauler that was laboring out of the planet's well, and pushed on into the upper atmosphere. He leveled out within the mesosphere and banked onto a northerly course that would take them over the target, the waves of gravitational distortion from the engines clearly visible as the ship plowed through the upper layers of the atmosphere.

"Weapons release in two," Kage said, never looking up from his displays as his four hands deftly manipulated the ship's controls. Two seconds later a weapons bay opened in the ship's belly and six missiles were spit out and sent on their way. Active telemetry began to come in from the missiles to Kage's terminal as they accelerated to hypersonic velocity and tracked for the target. Jason nudged the DL7 into a pursuit course and followed the missiles down towards the surface, the ship shuddering slightly as it muscled through the increasingly heavy atmosphere.

"Status," Jason said.

"We're still clean, no surface launches. All missiles tracking," Kage said. It was eleven seconds later when the missiles slammed straight down into the ground all around the compound, kicking up six impressive plumes of dirt and rock.

The missiles had been programmed to penetrate deep into the ground before the warheads detonated; their targets were the extensive underground facilities Doc knew were there. One missile malfunctioned and only five exploded, but the combined concussive force was sufficient to collapse large sections of the facility. The ground seemed to swallow up whole sections of the complex as if it were built over a sinkhole.

The gunship screamed over the city, decelerating violently as it came within range of the now smoking compound. The damage from the missiles was impressive, but they were taking no chances. Kage brought the ship's powerful main guns to bear and let loose a salvo of high-energy plasma that vaporized whole sections of the compound in a frightening display of destructive power. What wasn't destroyed instantly was flattened as the shockwave of superheated air from the plasma blasts slammed into it. Kage fired the main guns three more times before they overflew the site and Jason wrapped the big ship into a tight, right-hand turn. The ship groaned in protest as vapor poured off the wings from the sudden compression of the humid air during the high 'G' maneuver, but the effect on the crew was nullified by the artificial gravity generated by the deck plating. He angled his turn up slightly to gain some altitude and give them a better perspective for their second strafing run.

Although badly battered, the facility still had some teeth; three heavy particle beams lanced out from rooftop emplacements and impacted the ship's shields with spectacular results. Sparks exploded around the outside of the ship and alarms sounded as the shields fought to dissipate the energy from the beams. Jason aborted their run and yanked the ship into a vertical climb and went to full power. Even as the ship thundered into the sky, Kage was already targeting the beam emitters for their next run.

Jason kicked the ship into a left-handed hammerhead turn and put their nose back on the target. "Targets acquired and locked," Kage said. Jason accelerated savagely into a descending bank that would allow him to put their guns on target before coming into range of the particle cannons. Kage let loose with a full salvo from all the forward-facing weapons, resulting in an explosion that ripped the remaining buildings off their foundations and sent a massive plume of flame and debris right into their flight path.

"Shit!" Jason exclaimed, knowing it was too late to avoid it even as the DL7 plunged through the raining debris. Some of the impacts felt quite heavy as it shot out the other side and into the clear.

"We've got a ground car that escaped!" Kage shouted. "Two occupants, heading southwest away from the city."

"That'll be her! We need to stop that car, Commander," Doc said, speaking for the first time since the attack commenced. Jason fought the controls as he yanked the nose up and tried to bring the ship back around to track the ground vehicle. He actually had to switch flight modes and put the ship into a hover in order to pursue the comparatively slow ground vehicle.

"Take the road out in front of the car," Jason told Kage. A split second later the ship spat out an energy bolt that took out three lanes of roadway the car was traveling on. It instantly angled right onto a side street and accelerated away. Jason clumsily turned to pursue, the gunship wallowing in the low-speed maneuvering at the hands of a novice pilot. He swore to himself as the car took another turn and headed for a more populated area. "Disengage weapons, they're entering a populated area."

"We may need to risk it, Commander," Doc said from his station.

"You know I won't do that. Ground assault team, get ready." Jason goosed the ship ahead of the speeding car and swung back around to face it head-on, no small feat considering the size of the ship and the proximity of the buildings. He continued to descend, intent on forcing the car into stopping or risk running headlong into the mouth of the beast, so to speak.

His gamble paid off as the car swerved at the last minute and ran up onto a pedestrian walkway, jumping the curb and crashing through a large ground-level window. Jason was thankful that this particular ground car utilized wheels instead of hovering on repulsors; it was completely out of commission. "Crusher, you guys are up," Jason said as Kage opened the belly hatch that allowed Crusher and Lucky to fall in a controlled descent to the ground within a containment field. He watched on his display in awe as the pair sprinted into the building at incredible speed, both armed to the teeth. He climbed up and away from the street and swung over the building to avoid the risk of damaging the ship with a careless impact.

"It looks like they've escaped, Commander," Crusher reported. "The vehicle is empty and there's no sign of them." Doc slammed a fist onto his console and swore at that. "We're going to head to the roof of this building and see if we can run into them on the way up."

"Copy that, ground team. We'll move to—" Jason was cut off as the ship dipped and yawed to port.

"We're taking fire!" Kage said. "Looks like two law enforcement aircraft approaching to intercept us. Energy weapons only, shields holding."

"Damnit! Ground team, we're going to move away and try to elude our new friends. Try to make your way to the southern edge of this city block and wait for my call." Jason swung the ship around to the north and accelerated aggressively on a course that would force the intercepting aircraft to radically change direction to try and keep up.

"Acknowledged, Commander," Crusher said calmly as the gunship screamed over the city, terrifying the residents. Jason swung around wide over the city as he pushed the ship to supersonic speeds to shake off his pursuers, his course taking him out of the population center and over rolling agricultural fields. He dropped down closer to the ground to mask their sensor signature and banked into a large, sweeping turn that covered miles of ground until he was pointing back to the southern edge of the city.

The two pursuing ships were not fooled by the move. They were soon joined by two more aircraft and moved to cut them off. Jason calculated the odds and decided to take the risk, pushing their velocity up as high as he dared as he raced back to his two crewmates he had left behind. "Get ready to open the hatch and grab them," he said to Kage.

"Already on it. It's going to be close though," was the tense reply.

"I know. Can't be helped."

"We're in position, Commander," Crusher said over the open channel. "We're on the roof of the tallest building on the southern edge of the city block we inserted at." Kage quickly used their com signal to pinpoint their location and send a waypoint to Jason's display, allowing him to fly directly to them.

"Heads up, guys, we'll be coming in hot," Jason warned them. He came in as close as he dared before pulling the nose up and flaring, bleeding off speed and bringing the ship to a rough hover over the roof. Kage activated the containment field to pull them off the rooftop and into the ship as soon as Jason edged over into position.

"We've got them, securing hatch and bringing the ventral shields back up," Kage said. Jason hammered down on the controls and the ship surged forward just as the first shots from their pursuers began bouncing off the aft shields. The ship streaked through the sky and overflew the original target, now a smoking crater, one last time.

"Take a sensor sweep of the target, we'll analyze it later," he said as he climbed up and out of the city. As soon as they overflew the site, Jason didn't try to be creative in their escape; he pointed the nose of the gunship straight up and slammed the grav-drive to full power. It was only as they transitioned from the thermosphere into the exosphere that Jason began to unclench his muscles. There was no sign of pursuit from the surface and they hadn't detected any space-based defensive capability on the way in. For the moment it appeared they were safe.

Jason accepted the first waypoint from Kage's station and engaged the slip-drive while they were still in-system. Once the canopy darkened and the weapons were powered down, Jason could feel the tension in his neck and shoulders and the sweat that caused his shirt to cling to him. He looked around at his bridge crew, "Well, that didn't go exactly as planned."

"No, it didn't," Doc agreed, obviously frustrated as the rest of the crew made their way onto the bridge, including Twingo. "I'd feel better knowing we got her, but taking that facility out is a huge blow to their operation."

"And also painted a huge target on our backs," Twingo said.

"I'd say that was a given after The Vault—" Jason began, but was interrupted by an alert on his com panel. A slip-space communication was coming through, and it was specifically coming through to the ship's transponder code. Whoever it was knew exactly what ship they were contacting. With a feeling of dread, Jason activated the link and sent it to the main canopy display. He instantly regretted it as Bondrass' face appeared, larger than life, on the enormous display. The crime boss was enraged beyond description as his skin kept shifting colors and his eyes threatened to bulge from his head.

"YOU! Did you think you could steal from me and hide?!" Bondrass was screaming with barely contained fury. "You've sealed your fate! Where is Deetz?!" Jason looked at the others in confusion. Apparently Bondrass was behind on his intel.

"He's currently unavailable," Jason said blandly. "Would you like me to give him a message?" Bondrass screamed in wordless fury and lashed out at the display with his claws. While he was still spouting gibberish and baring his teeth, someone slipped him a tablet display with something written on it. The boss read it and paled instantly to a light green. He looked up at the camera with a look of shock and horror written on his face.

"What have you done? WHAT HAVE YOU DONE?!" Bondrass screamed. He pointed at Doc, "Do you understand what you've done?!"

"Completely," Doc said unflappably, walking into the video frame.

"I'm going to make you regret this," Bondrass hissed, focusing on him. "I'll keep you alive for decades so I can torture you slowly. I'll—" Lines of video interference ran through the feed as Bondrass and his aide seemed to sway on their feet. "What was that?"

"Sir, we're under attack!" The shout came from someone off screen as Bondrass' ship seemed to take several more heavy hits. The crime boss looked utterly confused.

"Why are they attacking me? Get me in touch with the other syndicate members, NOW!"

"Maybe you didn't pay your membership dues?" Jason suggested in a helpful tone. Bondrass snapped his head back to the display, seeming to have forgotten he had been talking to them.

"Did you have something to do with this!?"

"Well," Jason said as he scratched his head thoughtfully. "There may be some slight confusion as to who actually stole the cargo ship from The Vault. We *might* have sort of made it look like your security personnel shot the guards and made off with all that loot. Look, you seem really busy. Maybe you can call back when you're not so pressed for time?" Before Bondrass could reply, sparks and smoke began filling the bridge of his ship and the link suddenly terminated.

"Well," Twingo said with a broad smile, lacing his hands behind his head as he sprawled in one of the bridge seats, "that takes care of that."

"Hopefully," Jason said.

Chapter 20

Jason and Twingo stood watching the last cargo hauler roll away from the hangar and back towards the flight line. It had taken them a few weeks to fence all the stolen cargo they had liberated from The Vault in a manner which kept it all low-profile enough so the other crime bosses wouldn't hear about it. The precious metal had been easy enough, and a lot of the weaponry they decided not to keep wasn't easily traced, but the piles of printed currency had been problematic. Laundering a mountain of bills that had ID chips embedded in them hadn't been easy, but they eventually found a money launderer who was willing to take on the risk.

Looking back at the empty hangar they had used to stage all of their ill-gotten goods left Jason with a sense of finality. In a way, he was sorry to see this adventure come to an end. He had been beaten, threatened, terrified, sold ... but somewhere along the line he had rediscovered that spark within himself, that love of life he had lost. The thought of returning to his little cabin in the mountains to simply mark time alone was now incredibly unappealing. He looked up at the sky of Breaker's World and saw they were about to get rained on. "We'd better hustle unless we want to swim back," he said, slapping Twingo on the shoulder and walking back towards the far end of the space port.

The pair walked in silence, both lost in thought as they pondered what would happen to them now that they were finished with what they had set out to do. When they finally reached the far end of the complex, Jason broke into a smile as he caught sight of the sleek gunship. Like any man who had been through an incredible adventure with a particular machine, Jason felt an almost emotional bond with the Jepsen Aero DL7. It had kept them safe during their bungling rescue mission attempt and then provided the means with which to exact some measure of revenge on Bondrass. (Or complete revenge, depending on whether one believed the crime boss was actually dead. Jason wasn't so sure.) He didn't know where he would be going from there, but he knew he didn't want to leave it behind.

The other four crewmembers were standing under the ship's tail section as Jason and Twingo approached, just in time for the sky to open up with fat, painful raindrops. They all retreated up the ramp and stood at the mouth of the cargo bay as the rain soaked the ground and began to run off the ship in rivulets. They stood in silence for a few moments until Kage, the most high-strung among them, couldn't take it anymore.

"So, what's next?"

"I've wondered the same thing myself," Crusher said quietly. They lapsed back into an uncomfortable silence.

"Why don't we do this?" Twingo said, looking around at them.

"This what?" Jason asked.

"*This*. There are a lot of folks out there who have slipped through the cracks or have nobody to turn to, so many that live in fear and are ignored by uncaring or corrupt governments. We have a modest fortune, a unique skill set, and one badass warship," the engineer said, impassioned. "We could make it our job to make sure someone stands up for these people." When he finished, they all looked around at each other, hints of smiles tugging at the corners of mouths. They turned back to Jason, and he looked at each of them in turn, already knowing what his own choice was going to be.

"Well, I can't leave you lunatics to your own devices, that much is certain ... I'm in," he said to cheers and wide smiles.

"I am happy you've decided to continue leading us, *Captain*," Crusher said as he squeezed Jason's shoulder hard enough to make him grit his teeth. Kage edged over to the cargo bay computer terminal and started flying through menus and commands. Doc walked over and grabbed five more bottles of a local ale they had been drinking while the others began to discuss the details of their new arrangement. The computer's voice halted their conversation.

"Crew manifest update confirmed. Captain Jason Burke, commanding officer." They all looked over at Kage, who just smiled.

"Now it's official," he said, accepting a bottle of beer from Doc as he rejoined the group.

"You know," Twingo said. "We really should name her." He gestured around him at the ship. The others nodded their assent.

"Captain?" Doc asked. "What do you think?"

In truth, Jason had already been thinking about it for the last few days, afraid to say it out loud.

"In my world's mythology there's a creature, a bird actually, that is reborn in fire. It rises up from its own ashes. In a very real way, it's the same with all of us, and even the ship herself; we've all burned away our previous lives and have been reborn new. It's called the Phoenix," Jason said.

"A powerful name," Crusher approved. The others nodded as well.

"Am I to be included in this new unit?" Lucky asked suddenly, silent up to that point.

"You've earned a spot here, if you want it," Jason said. "But it's up to you. You're welcome to stay here as a crewmate and a friend for as long as you wish, and later if you decide you want to leave, we'll drop you off anywhere you want with your cut from the ship's treasury. The same goes for all of you. This is a strictly voluntary force."

"Thank you, Captain," Lucky said. "I would indeed like to stay and serve with you. All of you."

"Glad to have you," Jason said with a smile. He resisted the urge to shake the synth's hand; he wasn't sure Lucky's grip wouldn't accidentally crush all the bones in his own hand.

"So what are we going to be called? It's a little clunky to introduce ourselves as 'The Group of Guys Who Help People and Then Break Their Things,'" Kage said with a grin. They again deferred to Jason, watching him expectantly.

"You guys don't want to vote on any of this stuff?" he asked jokingly.

"While we're all friends, you're our commanding officer. Whatever this becomes will be molded by you, and the choices you make," Doc said seriously. Jason stared out at the heavy rain and took a long pull off his beer.

"Everything has a beginning and an end, an alpha and an omega," he said as he stared out over the spaceport, voicing a line of thought that had been in his head since they had landed. "By the time we have to get involved, it will be as a last resort for most, at the very end of hope for those that we'll encounter. Who we are should speak to that, both for the people we'll be helping and those we'll be helping them against." Captain Burke paused and looked his crew over again. This wasn't going to be an easy life they'd just signed up for, but it could be hugely rewarding if they had the dedication and mental toughness for it.

"Gentlemen, we are now Omega Force."

Epilogue:

Jason Burke shuffled out onto the back porch of his cabin and took in the view. It was late summer and the sun was just setting over the Rocky Mountains, splashing the sky with muted oranges and pinks. Beautiful. Being back on Earth had a surreal feel after what he had been through. It was as if he was now a stranger on his own world and he began to feel anxious to leave again. He had come back to get his personal belongings, but once he was back he realized that he didn't really have anything he wanted to take with him. He'd been hiding here for so long, just going through the motions of living … he'd not realized how empty his existence had become while wallowing in self-pity.

He felt like he'd been given a second chance with Omega Force. He had the ability to make a real difference again, but this time on his own terms. The same drive to serve that had made him enlist in the Air Force, and then volunteer for Special Forces in basic training, was pushing him again to embrace this new role. This time would be different though; as Captain of the *Phoenix* he would decide whom and what he would fight for. He would no longer be grist for the mill, risking his life for causes that weren't his own and a government that didn't care.

He sighed and turned to walk back inside, closing the door behind him. He had also come home to tie up any and all loose ends and was mildly depressed to find that he didn't really have all that many. The rest of the crew was doing the same, spread out among the stars, each closing out what remained of their former lives. They had flown to Pinnacle Station a couple weeks ago and the others had taken commercial flights to where they needed to go. Since Earth obviously had no flights available to it, Jason flew the *Phoenix* home.

He had no living family save for an aunt and uncle that lived in southern Oklahoma, but he hadn't spoken to them in years. The only thing he had in the world (at least this one) was a little bit of cash saved up from his active duty days, a beat-up truck that wasn't worth much, and the cabin his parents had left him long ago. He had written a letter to the only person left on the planet he cared about and left instructions on how to get to the property the cabin was on and how to go about legally claiming it. After debating on how much to say, he had settled on a simple "goodbye and good luck."

He eyed the two military duffle bags that were sitting on the living room floor, the sum of his worldly possessions, and then checked his watch. The *Phoenix* was sitting in high orbit waiting to hear from him. He hadn't wanted to risk it being discovered by leaving it grounded while he took care of his business. When it was dark enough he'd access the ship via his neural implant and have it come and get him. He would be a few days early to Pinnacle by leaving that night, but he didn't have any reason to hang around on Earth.

He heard the front door to the cabin open on squeaky hinges and, expecting the worst, spun around to face whatever was coming in. When he saw who it was, his heart began to hammer in his chest almost painfully, but not from fear. Standing in the doorway, blonde hair framed by the fading light of day, was her. She stood there, as beautiful as ever, his one true regret.

"Hi, Jason," she said softly. "I got your letter."

Maybe the guys will be waiting at Pinnacle for me instead.

Thank you for reading *Omega Rising*.

If you enjoyed the story, Captain Burke and the guys will be back in:

Omega Force: Soldiers of Fortune.

Follow me on Facebook and Twitter for the latest updates:

www.facebook.com/joshua.dalzelle

@JoshuaDalzelle

65419785R00114

Made in the USA
Lexington, KY
11 July 2017